Y0-AAT-444

Listen while I tell of the story of the beginning, of the darkness which was broken by the shattering of the Great Egg, of the tribulations of those cursed by their own pride and the terrible fate which they met beyond the edge of time. Lo, these things I tell are written in the stars and to be read in the Omphalos, the heart of all things....

PAWN OF
THE OMPHALOS

E.C. Tubb

FAWCETT GOLD MEDAL • NEW YORK

PAWN OF THE OMPHALOS

Copyright © 1980 E.C. Tubb

All rights reserved

Published by Fawcett Gold Medal Books, a unit of CBS Publications, the Consumer Publishing Division of CBS Inc.

All the characters in this book are fictitious, and any resemblance to actual persons living or dead is purely coincidental.

ISBN: 0-449-14377-5

Printed in the United States of America

First Fawcett Gold Medal printing: December 1980

10 9 8 7 6 5 4 3 2 1

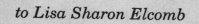

to Lisa Sharon Elcomb

1

FROM a distance it was a bright shimmer hanging in space which seemed to change so that each who saw it found a different shape: a ball, a cage, a cluster of pearls, a cone, a maze, the likeness of beasts. A thousand descriptions all adding to the same. A mystery. The Unknown.

Closer and the enigma grew. Details which should have been plain remained invisible, the surface a blazing mass of convoluted radiance which defied understanding. A baffling problem to the scientists, a fascinating spectacle to the tourists who came to Krait.

"It is a contradiction in time and space," said the guide. He was tall, lean, muffled in heavy garments. A native of the Ophidian worlds with slotted eyes and a skin bearing vestigial scales, sensitive to the cold despite the beamed heat bathing the area. "No one knows exactly what it is. Ships have tried to traverse it but none have returned."

Mark Carodyne said, "Destroyed?"

The guide shrugged. "As I said, no one knows. Probes cease to signal once they enter it. Manned vessels sent to investigate have not returned. No wreckage has even been discovered. Ships and crew have simply disappeared."

A girl shivered and moved closer to where Carodyne stood on the observation platform. "And it is coming towards us?"

"No, madam." The guide was patient. "The Omphalos does not move. That, among other things, is what makes it so unusual. It is stationary in relation to the universe and does not participate in the galactic drift."

A woman said, sharply, "Are we in danger? Could it swallow us as it did the ships you mentioned?"

"Krait is in no danger, madam," said the guide firmly. "It is coming closer, true, but we shall pass it at a safe distance. Now, if you will all turn your heads a little so as to look sidewise at the Omphalos without trying to focus your eyes, you may see something very interesting."

Dutifully the party obeyed, all but Carodyne, who had no time for visual tricks. Thoughtfully he stared directly at the patch of glowing luminescence. It was too large to take in as a whole, and he studied it as he would Earth's moon, letting his eyes drift over the surface. There was a crater—or was it? There a string of glowing spheres like a row of pearls. A ray of startling brilliance suddenly appeared converging on another to form—what? They vanished as he tried to fit a recognizable picture to the pattern. Again he caught the hint of something familiar. A mountain range? A mesh of rivers? The circuitry of an electronic device? It was gone before he could decide and he caught the impression of a bird, wide-winged, crested and with an open beak. It dissolved in a shimmer as if clouds were parting to reveal fitful gleams edged with pluming smoke.

The colors were too bright, the patterns changing too rapidly for him to make sense of what he saw. The thing was a kaleidoscope of eye-burning sharpness and hypnotic enticement, and he blinked, seeing dancing retinal images which added to the confusion.

Beside him the girl sucked in her breath. "Artelle," she murmured. "But it can't be!"

A matron cried out, "Sonhed! My baby!"

An elderly man shook his head and rubbed at his eyes. Tears wetted his cheeks. "No," he whispered. "She's gone. I don't want to be hurt again. The memory—"

Mark felt the girl grip his arm. "I saw it," she said blankly. "Artelle, the house where I was born. But it was destroyed ten years ago when I was a child. Yet it was there exactly as I remembered it."

"No," he said flatly. "It was a trick of the light. Have you never looked into a leaping flame and seen pictures among the coals? A wood fire, perhaps, while out hunting? The big

8

one at the lodge? The eye is baffled with continually changing perspectives and the mind tries to rationalize the signals it receives in terms of familiar images. Look again, all you'll see is a mass of shifting color."

"But it was so real," she insisted. "So very real."

To her and to the others of the party, each seeing what they longed to find, a home, a lost child, a remembered romance, a dream, perhaps, created from shifting light and imagination.

In the car which carried them back to the lodge she introduced herself. "I'm Shara Mordain of Elgesh," she said. "And you're Mark Carodyne. I saw you when you arrived. Are you alone?"

"Yes."

"I'm glad of that," she said with naked candor. "I would rather not have to fight for you. Have you been to Elgesh?"

"No."

"We have two women for every man and so we have to do the chasing. Do you mind?"

He smiled as he looked down at her where she sat close beside him on the seat. Her face, framed in the thick fur collar of her robe, was strongly boned, the cheeks high, the nostrils flared a little, the lips full over a determined jaw. Beneath the robe he could sense the long lines of her body, the softness and strength of a female animal. She would have money, be wilful and could be a problem if he permitted it.

Quietly he said, "Tell me about Elgesh."

"There isn't much to tell. It's just another world like most of the rest. We had a virus disease hit us awhile ago. A wild mutant which attacked the prostate and affected the testicles. Within two years ninety percent of our men were sterile. That wouldn't have mattered too much but the birthrate went all to hell. Five girls for every boy. We're leveling out now but things will never be the same."

"And you?"

She hesitated and then said, "I know what you're thinking. A man-hungry girl on the hunt. Well, maybe you're right, but I don't like to think so. Just call it a reactive syndrome caused by early conditioning and leave it at that." She

9

glanced through the window at the blur of light in the sky. "What did you think of it?"

"The Omphalos?" He shrugged. "I told you. It's just a giant kaleidoscope."

"Don't let the guide hear you call it that. I don't think he'd like it. They say his people used to worship it years ago. They called it the 'mirror of the mind' or something like that. They even thought that mysterious gods lived there and controlled their lives every inch of the way. I'll even bet they sacrificed to it if the crops or weather was bad."

"They wouldn't be unusual if they had," he said. "It's the normal progression of peoples rising from the primitive levels towards civilization. On Earth they used to offer sacrifices to the moon and the sun as well as to the soil and the sea. Insurance against bad climates and poor crops. All races have done the same."

"Earth, you come from there?"

"Yes."

"The home planet," she said. "One day I'm going to see it. Is it as beautiful as they claim?"

"I think so."

"You're biased. Are you an anthropologist?"

"What makes you think that?"

"You seem to know all about religions and primitive peoples. Are you?"

"No."

"How do you know about them then?"

"I read a lot."

"Men!" she said with repressed fury. "What's the matter with you all? The ones I can't stand never stop talking and the ones I like never begin. All right, I'll do it the hard way. Question and answer. If you're not an anthropologist what are you?"

"A gambler," he said, and rose to his feet as the car slid to a halt at the foot of the ramp leading to the lodge.

Inside it was warm with a glitter of polished copper, polished wood, a great fire burning in a stone surround, rugs scattered over the wooden floor. The lights were subdued and set in lanterns of hammered iron, more strung on the rafters, still more on the cornices. It was the idealized version of a

10

winter shelter, a pleasant haven from the snow and ice and winter skies outside. A servant came bustling forward with a tray heavy with goblets, the traditional greeting cup of Krait, a light wine spiced with pungent flavors heated over an open fire.

The party drank in silence, most still bemused by what they had seen. Shara opened her robe and fanned herself with a slender hand. Beneath the thick material she wore a clinging form-fit of scarlet and gold.

"I'm too warm for comfort, Mark. I'll have to get into something cooler. See you later?"

"Perhaps."

She was direct. "Why the hesitation? Don't you like me or is it that you don't want to get involved?"

"Yes and no," he said bluntly. "I like you and I don't want to get involved. In any case I've work to do."

"Gambling?"

"That's right."

"I thought you were joking," she said slowly. "Giving me a flip answer. You don't look like a gambler."

"All life is a gamble, Shara. Everything you do is taking a chance of some kind. And when you take a chance you can't afford distractions."

Nor complications, he thought as he watched her leave and walk to the wide staircase which led to the upper chambers. A rich and spoiled young woman always spelled potential danger. She would demand her own way and be difficult when she didn't get it. He turned as a hand touched his arm. The man was short, round and looked like an inflated balloon, but Carodyne wasn't deceived. Presh was the product of a heavy planet and the apparent fat was highly developed muscle.

"Everything is prepared, sir," he said quietly. "If you are ready to commence, my master is at your disposal."

Tagh Altin, the Ekal of Kotan, was a small, wizened man with a narrow face, beaked nose and a fanatical love of chess. He waited in a private annex off the main chamber, the board set ready before him. He smiled as Carodyne approached.

"It is good of you to accommodate an old man at his simple pleasure, Mark. A thousand?"

11

High stakes on a single game—more than high when it represented almost all his wealth, but Carodyne nodded, casually, as if he had expected a higher wager.

"As you wish, my lord."

"Then it is settled. Some refreshment perhaps before we begin? No? Then let us decide the first move."

The board was of gold and silver, the pieces of emerald and ruby. Carodyne picked up a pawn of each, manipulated them behind his back, held out his closed hands. Shrewd eyes studied his face as the Ekal reached a thin hand towards them. It drifted towards the left, hesitated, moved to the right and then, like a striking bird of prey, moved back to the left, touching like a withered leaf.

"It is your move first, my lord." Carodyne replaced the pieces, his face impassive. He had forced the choice with a carefully calculated flicker of the eyes. A small gain but the final victory could depend on such accumulations.

The game commenced. The Ekal moved his pieces with hesitation, lingering, pursing his lips and frequently tugging at the lobe of his right ear. Carodyne moved with quick precision, acting as though he followed a preconceived plan. Both men lied with every move they made. The Ekal had no need to act like a fumbling beginner, and Carodyne had no plan, playing as much by instinct as inspiration. He could play the game and play it well, but he was not playing simple chess. He was playing against a man who played chess. There was a difference.

"A fascinating game," murmured Tagh Altin. "No one can tell how old it is. At my palace I have a thousand sets each different yet all basically the same. Men carved from wood, from stone, metal and seeds. Boards made of as many materials, some of them decorated with fantastic designs. One day you must see them." He moved a piece, removed another. "You were careless, Mark. Already you are weakened."

Carodyne moved without comment.

"I hear that you have seen the Omphalos," continued the Ekal. "You found it intriguing?"

"Interesting." Carodyne moved a castle. "An oddity of nature."

12

"As is life itself—or so certain philosophers would have us believe. So many worlds and so many races, but each holding disturbing similarities. A matter of chance? Perhaps, but there are those who would have us believe it is more than that. A matter of calculation, they say. Who can tell?"

The words were a screen to mask thoughts and provide distraction. Carodyne ignored them, concentrating on the board. The pattern shown was almost classical and, if continued, would lead to his inevitable defeat. He must break it, shatter the attack and launch one of his own. Not a neat, textbook series of moves which could be matched and countered, but a blasting away of threatening pieces and the opening out of the game. Not typical chess, perhaps, but good survival tactics.

"You know, Mark," said Tagh Altin as the game progressed, "I have often thought this a game with far wider implications than we realize. Take the men we move. Isn't it true that, in a way, we control their destiny? We save them, sacrifice them, use them as we will. Suppose they had individual awareness? Can you accept the premise?"

Carodyne moved a bishop and took a knight.

"A dead man," mused the Ekal. He had stopped tugging at his ear. "Or a man wrenched from his own time and place. Lifted from the sight of his companions, torn from a familiar environment and thrown elsewhere. Often I dream of a master chess player manipulating the worlds of men. Sometimes, in that dream, I am the player." He reached forward and captured the offending bishop.

Carodyne said, quietly, "As you saw in the Omphalos, my lord?"

He had scored. He could tell it at the sharp intake of breath, the momentary tension. Immediately he launched his attack.

"I think we all have these delusions of grandeur. A psychologist would call it wish fulfillment, or perhaps an attempt to compensate on a subconscious level for imagined inadequacy." He moved his other bishop. "Your move, my lord."

He gave the man no time to think. As the thin hand hesitated he said, "Or again such dreams could be the result of a deep sense of guilt. A desire to justify reprehensible deeds

13

by the adoption of a cloak of omnipotence. God can do no wrong. Therefore, if we can convince ourselves that we are God, then obviously we could have done no wrong."

The Ekal moved, making a bad mistake. Carodyne swept up the exposed piece.

"A flagrant attempt at self-justification, my lord, as I am sure you will agree. A deed, once done, cannot be turned into something other than it was at the time of its doing. In many ways the Omphalos could be likened to a mirror in which each man can read his soul. You have moved, my lord?"

Fifteen minutes later Carodyne knew that he had won. The Ekal had been shaken, careless beyond recovery, and soon would be forced to admit defeat. He stared at the board, his hand tugging at his ear as Carodyne relaxed for the first time since commencing the game. Idly he looked around.

The annex was almost full.

Aside from Presh, standing close beside his master, a dozen men and women stood around looking on. He caught a glimpse of Shara Mordain, a glitter of gemmed scarlet and silken flesh. Her hair was plaited and crested high over the face, a mane so black that it held blue shimmers. Her figure was as he'd imagined, soft and strong and undeniably female. He gave her one glance then returned his attention to the board.

Victory was his—if he wanted it.

He lifted his eyes and stared directly at the Ekal. Tagh Altin seemed to have shrunk a little, one finger riding at the side of his nose, the hand a mask, perhaps, for the lips beneath. The eyes too were a mask, emotionless, almost unseeing, yet aware of the watching men and women, their intangible hunger to see him defeated, beaten, his pride in tatters.

They lowered a little, met those of the man facing him across the board, held for a long, intense moment.

Carodyne said quietly, "My lord, if I may impose on your generosity? A glass of wine?"

The finger fell away from the nose and the eyes widened a little. Then they were once again a mask yet they were not as they had been, and something had left the small figure perched on the chair. Fear, perhaps? Tension, certainly.

14

"My dear, Mark. Of course. Presh, bring a bottle of the finest vintage."

The wine was cool, sweet, refreshing to the tongue. Carodyne swallowed half the glass, watching as the Ekal followed suit. Now, his decision made, he could afford to be careless. Yet even so the game had to be played out. It was not enough to lose, he had to make it appear that he fought every step of the way.

Tagh Altin said, "It is your move, I think."

Carodyne lifted a piece, set it down. "Check, my lord."

A simple check and one easy to block. A skilled player would notice the mistake, not obviously bad but bad enough to signal the inevitable. Five moves, he thought. Seven at the most. The Ekal would have reason to boast his victory.

It took six. A happy compromise.

2

OUTSIDE the annex the large, communal room was filling with a crowd of variegated types: a small group of Dinwee from the Ebon cluster, brightly clothed, lithe as cats, their enormous eyes shielded against the too-bright lighting; some Lapash, tall, arrogant, strutting in glinting mail with daggers at their belts, a startling contrast to a party of Pilms, drab in their brown robes. Others from a dozen divergent races, milling, filling the air with the blur of conversation. Waiters hurried past bearing trays of drinks and snacks and the long bar was thronged. A normal, late-night scene at the lodge.

A stocky man called from a group of others. He was dressed in stained leather touched with blue, his face scarred and his big hands dwarfing the mug he held.

"Bad luck, Mark. I hope it isn't an omen."

"Don't lie, Helm," said one of his companions. "You hope that Mark's on the skids, we all do. Nothing personal, Mark, but every little helps."

Helm Fendhal shrugged. "On the slope anything can happen. Tonight we drink, tomorrow how many will be smears on the ice?" The thought disturbed him and he lifted his mug, slamming it down empty and bellowing for a refill. He was drinking too much, cursed, perhaps, by his tendency to see omens in every event. Whatever the reason he was being unwise. "You'll join us, Mark?"

Details could be learned in unguarded moments, and it would be impolitic to refuse. Carodyne lifted his mug, barely wetting his lips. "Any news of the weather?"

"It'll be a perfect day," said another of the group. "A slight overcast, no wind to speak of, and no snow. One of us should set a new record."

"I hear that Cran is having trouble with his ship," said a tall Venedian. Like Carodyne he only pretended to drink. "And Igal had a doctor in to see him. Rumor has it that his heart is playing up."

"That or his feet are getting cold." Helm gulped at his mug. "Igal should have quit long ago. He's past it. Slow reflexes and too high a regard for his skin. What do you think, Mark?"

Carodyne shrugged. "Tomorrow will tell."

"Tomorrow we'll be either rich, broke, crippled or dead," said Helm somberly. "Well, to hell with it. Let's enjoy life while we've the chance."

The philosophy of those who made a living by risking their lives—or the escape of a man who had pushed his luck too far and knew, deep inside, that he had nothing left to give. A friend would have drugged Fendhal, keeping him from the race and saving his life at the expense of his friendship, but here there were no friends. Beneath the conviviality and banter lay the rock-hard determination of men selfish to the extreme. To them only one thing mattered, to win the coming race, and if the knives they used to weaken the opposition were invisible, they were nonetheless real.

Carodyne edged from the group as the talk and drinking

16

continued. Fendhal was out. Igal was probably playing a deceptive game, summoning a doctor so that rumor would cause the others to underestimate his danger. The Venedian was an unknown quality, young, sharp, cunning as he steered surmise and speculation. The others? Carodyne watched, assessing each from small, unconscious betrayals.

He set down the mug and turned, seeing Shara Mordain coming towards him. Their eyes met and she said, "You lied to me, Mark. Why didn't you tell me you were a professional skimmer?"

"I'm not."

"But you're racing tomorrow."

"One race. A gamble that I'll walk off with the prize. I didn't lie."

"No?" She tilted her head a little so as to stare into his face. "Perhaps not, but if you're a gambler why did you deliberately lose back there?"

"Did I?"

"I've played chess since I was five. You had the Ekal beaten when you asked for that wine. And then you lost. I'd like to know why."

Verandahs ringed the lodge, small, intimate places closed with transparent panels, warm and snug against the cold outside. He led her to one and closed the door. In the clear air the stars shone like jewels, the flaring luminescence of the Omphalos dominating the night.

"Mark?"

Coldly he said, "You don't look like a fool so why act like one? The Ekal is a powerful man. He wouldn't thank you if he learned you were spreading a stupid rumor."

"Is that why you brought me in here? To talk unheard?" She shrugged as he made no comment. "I'd hoped that—well, never mind. In any case you needn't worry. I'm not totally a fool. It's just that I was curious as to why you did it. More than curious, Mark. I must know."

"Must?"

She said, as if she hadn't caught the sharpness in his tone, "Let me guess. The Ekal is rich and proud and old. He has one passion in life that you know of, the game of chess. Unfortunately to love a thing isn't enough to become truly pro-

17

ficient at it. He is a good player, agreed, but there are better. You could be one of them, or at least as good. You could have beaten him and then what? You would have won the bet."

"I didn't win."

"You could have done, but, if you had, he would have lost more than money. He would have lost his pride. You knew that. And he knew it. Knew that you had him beaten. And then, somehow, he knew what you intended to do. But how?" She paused and then, "The wine," she decided. "When you asked for it he knew. The rest was just to save his face. But why, Mark? I can understand you being diplomatic, even considerate, but to throw away a thousand? Do you really trust in the gratitude of princes?"

"I am a gambler, Shara, not a fool."

"Of course not," she said. "A man from nowhere taking on the best in a crazy sport. Ready to ride down the side of a mountain in a tiny ship with death waiting if you make the slightest error. All right, I know you've won the chance by showing what you can do at the trials. And you don't seem to worry that fifty percent of all who start will get killed before the finish. But why do it, Mark? For what? Glory?"

"The money," he said. "The prize. Who can spend glory?"

"I don't think you mean that. Not in the way it sounds. You're not a greedy man in the usual sense of the word. If so you'd have beaten the Ekal and taken his money and to hell with his pride. So why are you doing it? For fun? For experience?"

Dryly he said, "I don't lack experience in handling ships."

"Then what do you hope to gain?"

He ignored the question, looking instead at the Omphalos. It seemed to writhe, to shift and blaze with a sudden, inner brilliance. Beside him the girl sucked in her breath.

"It's beautiful," she whispered. "But, somehow, terrible at the same time. Frightening even, and dangerous. I was talking to a man, Nev Chalom, you know him?"

"No."

"A very clever man, an astrophysicist and mathematician from Ulate. He has a theory that the Omphalos is not as stable as people think. He claims that, at times, it pulses, expands so as to engulf everything in a wide area. That it

18

could have started much smaller than we see it now and, over eons of time, grown to the size we see. Does that make sense, Mark?"

"Any theory makes sense until observed fact makes it false."

"You're fencing with me," she said. "But imagine it, we are standing here, assuming that we are perfectly safe and then, all of a sudden, the Omphalos spreads out to swallow this world. What would happen to the people on it? Would they be destroyed?"

He shrugged, not answering.

"And the ships, Mark," she murmured. "You heard what the guide said. What happens to the ships and men who vanished? Are they inside there somewhere, perhaps waiting for someone to rescue them? Sometimes I—" She broke off, her breath a sharp sibilance. "Mark!"

"What is it?"

"A face," she said. "I saw a face!"

Truth or lie he had no way of telling, but her hands shook as he gripped them in his own and little quivers ran over her body.

"Imagination," he said. "I told you before, look long enough and you will see anything you wish. A face, a dream, the terrors of childhood."

"It was so real," she whispered. "And so—not evil—but mocking. As if someone had looked through a curtain gloating at what it saw."

The management had provided entertainment. As they returned to the communal room the sound of pipes and drums rose above the muted blur of conversation. The pipes shrilled, high, thin, keening as they echoed from the low rafters, the drums were the monotonous beating of a heart, rolling with sonorous undertones. The dancers, three lithe girls, moved to the beat, sinuous, seeming to glide over the floor, bare feet adorned with paint and tufts of feather.

"A depiction of the spring festival," murmured a waiter as they joined the watchers. "In the old days they would have danced until only one remained alive. She would have been feted as a queen."

"To be ritually slain in the autumn," said Carodyne. "So

19

that her flesh and blood would give the soil strength to last the winter."

"You have knowledge of our ways, sir." The waiter, a native, stared at the tall man with respect. "Not many who come to Krait would know as much."

Shara said, "Do the old customs survive? I mean really survive?"

A veil dropped over the slotted eyes. "I do not understand, madam. Could I get you refreshment?"

"Later," said Carodyne. "After the dance. It would be a crime to cause a distraction."

The performance ended with a clash of cymbals. The dancers spun, stooping to gather the coins showered at their feet, smiling, skins glowing with sweat and oil. An old man took their place, his skin dull, his eyes thick with opaque film. He squatted, tapping on a gourd, his thin voice surprisingly clear.

"Listen while I tell of the story of the beginning, of the darkness which was broken by the shattering of the Great Egg, of the tribulations of those cursed by their own pride and the terrible fate which they met beyond the bend of time. Lo, these things I tell are written in the stars and to be read in the Omphalos, the heart of all things..."

A storyteller, poor contrast to the dancers and of little interest to the majority in the room. The thin voice became blurred by the rising hum of conversation.

Shara clung tightly to Carodyne's arm. "That poor man. He must feel terrible at being so ignored."

"He has his audience." Carodyne gestured to where the Pilms had gathered in a tight circle around the speaker. "They like primitive ways and he probably reminds them of home. They will listen and he will get his reward."

"And you, Mark?"

A roar echoed before he could make a reply. Helm Fendhal, shouting, staggered from the group of skimmers. He was red-faced, his big hands clenched in anger.

"You scut! You slimy Venedian toad! You filth! Branco was a friend. He lived like a man and he died like one. To call him a cheating coward—by God, I'll kill you for that!"

Trouble, flaring from overtense nerves and too much alcohol. The group dissolved as Helm advanced on the Venedian intent on murder. The man backed a little, his hand twitching at his sleeve. Metal glinted as he produced a knife.

"Mark!" Shara's hand was tight on his arm. "Why don't they stop it?"

The unthinking question of a fool. Let the competition eliminate itself and the race would be that much easier to win. They stood watching as the Venedian tensed himself, the knife held like a sword in his hand. A slash would be enough. Cut muscles would be as effective as a kill, and, if he used the blade, there would be questions to answer and, perhaps, disqualification from the race.

A man called, "Five to one on the Venedian." Lucas Marsh, a man who would bet on anything. "Quick now, five will get you one if the Venedian wins. Any takers?"

Carodyne jerked his arm free of the girl's grip, his hand dipping, rising with an empty mug, lifting, poising and throwing all in one swift motion. It flew across the room and smashed against the blade of the knife tearing it from the Venedian's hand. He jumped back, startled, then ran for the stairs.

"Coward!" yelled Fendhal after him. "Dirty, stinking coward! Now all of you drink to Branco. Drink, I say." He staggered and almost fell as he reached for his mug.

"A fool." Marsh shrugged as he spoke to Carodyne. "I wouldn't give fifty to one on his chances. But you've made an enemy, Mark. You'll have to watch out on the slopes tomorrow."

"Is that unusual?"

"No." Marsh lowered his voice. "Do you want me to act for you? Now is a good time. The odds have lengthened since you lost to the Ekal. You know how gamblers are, once a man starts to lose they think he will lose all the way. And you're unknown on Krait. An outsider. Well?"

"Later."

"But not too late," urged Marsh. "I can't place a bet without the cash. Let me have it and I'll get you the best price going."

He moved away, smiling, a man who lived by a careful

balancing of the odds, a gambler who took no chances and who rarely lost.

"I don't like him," said Shara. "He reminds me of a leech. Mark, I'm tired. Take me to my room."

It was warm, soft, the wide bed bright with a silken coverlet, the air heavy with the scent of her perfume. Little touches had made it a home; a doll with a battered face and hair of flaming red; a crystaline posey, the flowers looking dewy fresh; a mobile which turned in a glow of ever-changing light and which emitted a delicate chiming.

"On Elgesh there are winds which always blow and we hang sheets of crystal in the trees. I leave it on when I go out so that I shall always be reminded of home when I return. Do you think me sentimental, Mark?"

"There is nothing wrong in that."

"Or in reaching out for what you want?"

"No."

"Then reach, Mark. To the victor the spoils and you have won—need I tell you what?" She smiled as he shook his head. "You know, back there on the verandah, you had me worried. I began to feel as if I'd lost all my attraction. You know what happens on Elgesh in such a case?"

"You take ship," he said curtly. "You go hunting."

"The smart ones, yes," she admitted. "Those not so smart do other things. There are ways to reduce the demands of the body, but that wasn't for me." She lifted her hands to the crested hair and did something so that it fell in a rippling waterfall over her back and shoulders. "You know, Mark, you're a mystery. You say that you're a gambler but you don't look like one."

"No?"

"You look more like a wrestler. A fighter. A leader of men. On Elgesh we have wide oceans and rough seas. There are men who man the ships and some of them look a little like you. Tall and hard with eyes which see more than is obvious. Damn you, Mark. Do I have to beg?"

"Good night, Shara."

"What?" She stared her disbelief. "You really mean that?"

"I mean it."

She said, as he reached the door. "Wait! You don't trust

me, is that it? You think that I want to weaken you in some way, ruin your sleep, take the fine edge off your concentration so that you'll lose the race tomorrow. Give you drugged wine, perhaps. Other things. Must you be so cautious? Can't you take the chance that I am exactly what I seem?"

"No."

"But—"

"Good night, Shara."

Back in his room Carodyne stripped and showered and lay on the bed watching the shifting light on the ceiling, the glow of the Omphalos coming through the parted curtains of his window. The phone rang and he ignored it. It rang twice more and he hit the disconnect button. Fifteen minutes later someone knocked on his door. It was Presh summoning him to the Ekal.

3

"COINCIDENCE," mused Tagh Altin. "Despite all mathematical improbability it happens and, when it does, we can only be thankful to the fates which made it possible." He sat in the private room of his suite looking older, more fragile in his simple robe than he had when playing in the annex below. His chessboard stood beside him and, as Carodyne glanced at it, he said, "Mark, why did you let me win that game?"

"A gamble, my lord. I trust you to be generous."

"I shall not claim the wager, naturally. In fact I shall give you double what you would have lost, but is that all? Was your only reason to save an old man's pride?"

Carodyne said, bluntly, "You are rich and powerful, my lord. Your patronage would be of value."

"You are clever, Mark. A quality I regard as being most important when it comes to assessing a man. You are clever and have a coldly calculating determination which I can only admire. If I offered you employment would you accept it?"

"That depends on what it is, my lord."

"Something well within the reach of your skills. If you accept you will not race tomorrow. Instead I will give you five times the value of the prize. A fortune." Tagh Altin rose. "I shall not ask you to decide immediately. First I want you to meet someone. Nev Chalom."

"Of Ulate?"

"You know him?"

"I have heard of him, my lord."

"A brilliant man. You will be interested in what he has to say." The Ekal paused then added, "Interested and, I hope, intrigued."

Nev Chalom sat at a wide desk in a cluttered room attached to the Ekal's suite, a thin man with snapping eyes and a mouth which looked as if he had tasted something bad. Before him lay a mass of charts, graphs, computations bright with a dozen colors. His clothing was rumpled and his hair, thin and showing the scalp beneath, was in wild disarray.

He was checking a list of figures as they entered and continued to work, not looking up until he had flung down the sheet.

Tagh Altin said, "Chalom, meet Mark Carodyne."

"The skimmer?"

"He was to race, yes."

"Will race—unless I accept your proposition, my lord." Carodyne was firm. "As yet I don't know what it is."

"Which is why you are here. Chalom?"

"Explanations," grumbled the man. "Very well, my lord, I will do my best." To Carodyne he said, abruptly, "What do you know of the Omphalos?"

"Very little."

"And most of it surmise, I guess. Well, let me tell you what is really known about it. It is stationary to the galactic drift and this leads us to the conclusion that, at one time, it could have been at the actual center of our galaxy. I believe this is so. I also believe that it's not stable. Let me illustrate."

24

He unrolled a chart and tapped it with a finger.

"See? This is the Omphalos. This is the path the galaxy has taken past it. Extrapolating along the line of the galactic drift we find that several worlds are not where they should be. You are familiar with Holman's rule of stars?"

"No."

"A mathematical formula which determines the density of stars and their accompanying worlds. The stars are as they should be, the worlds are not. The reason could be that, at intervals, the Omphalos has pulsed, expanded so as to engulf the missing worlds. You follow?"

Carodyne stared at the chart. "There could be another explanation. The worlds could have drifted into the Omphalos."

"Yes," said the Ekal. "So I believe." He stilled Chalom's protest with a lifted hand. "My dear Nev, you are clever, that no one denies, but you also tend to blind and baffle with your science. Mark is a man of imagination, of action and instinctive response. Which is why he is here. Now begin again, and this time remember that you are not lecturing a class or talking to a fool."

Chalom was sullen. He said, "My lord, I am at your service, but some things cannot be divorced from scientific terminology. I have spent my life studying the Omphalos; I cannot condense the discoveries into a brief resume."

"You can," said the Ekal. He still smiled but now there was no humor in his eyes. "And you will."

To help the man Carodyne said, "I know the basics, or at least I know what is held to be the basic mystery of the Omphalos. It is impenetrable."

"Not so." Chalom caught at the lifeline. "It can be penetrated easily enough, the trouble is that something happens when a ship passes the barrier. Just what is the mystery. Probes have been sent with transmitting apparatus which ceases to transmit once past the determining line. Other instruments have monitored them. Now, if the probes had been destroyed there must have been a release of energy. No such release has been noted. Atomic bombs have been sent with timed detonators but with the same result. Either the bombs did not explode or, somehow, the released energy was con-

25

tained. If the Omphalos obeyed natural law this simply could not have happened. The surmise is that either the barrier contains a foreign region of space or, somehow, the probes and missiles were transmitted elsewhere. The first surmise I think we can take for granted. The second?" He shrugged. "That is what we are still trying to find out."

"And the manned vessels?"

Chalom hesitated. "As yet none have returned."

Carodyne examined the chart, paying no attention to the mass of lines, the involved formulae, but using the act as an excuse to remain silent. There was a tension in the room which had not been there earlier as if something had been touched on and a reaction expected.

Tagh Altin said, quietly, "Aren't you interested, Mark?"

"In what, my lord?"

"The manned vessels which have vanished. We know of seven expeditions and how many before that, ships which hit the Omphalos by accident or curiosity, no one can guess. You mentioned them, I thought you could have a reason."

"The best, my lord. You mentioned employment. If it is your intention to ask me to follow them I am not interested. There are easier ways to die."

"We don't know they are dead," said Chalom quickly. "There is no way of telling." He glanced at the Ekal then continued, in a rush of words, "The first four followed a pattern. Each thought the other must have failed in some way, engine breakdown, failure of the communication equipment, anything. Or perhaps they just didn't believe what they were told. The next was an expedition from Ulate, the first, and it held special equipment. Automatic signaling devices, new shielding and more powerful engines. The crew was conditioned under a dozen hypnotic safeguards to return immediately at the slightest sign of danger. A web of deep-buried commands which were designed to operate on the subconscious level and which should not have failed. Apparently it was not enough. The ship vanished like the others."

"The sixth was from Kotan," said the Ekal bleakly. "Three men relying on drugs to maintain optimum mental facilities while their ship drifted on automatic withdrawal control in the path of the Omphalos. Direct radio communication was maintained to a monitoring vessel, and an unbroken commentary continued. It broke off in the middle of a word. For the rest—nothing."

"The last was from Ulate again." Chalom paced to the desk, returned, stood beside the Ekal. "Four men, one of them a telepath from Eem, a mutant with a high degree of sensitivity who remained in rapport with his mate carried on a supporting vessel. The mate went insane. The ship vanished."

As ships would continue to vanish, thought Carodyne. Ships and men as long as the race was cursed with the driving need to know, to understand, to probe the unknown.

Quietly he said, "There is a story told in the villages of Pholon about a tribe which hoped to catch a moon. They could see it clearly, floating in the waters of a lake. The lake was very deep but the people of the tribe were very determined. Many drowned but still they kept trying. Now the tribe no longer exists but the moon still shines in the water."

The Ekal was sharp. "Meaning?"

"It is wise for a man to recognize his limitations. Seven expeditions have tried to solve the secret of the Omphalos. How many more must vanish before you give up?"

"Did I say we were trying?"

"Will you say, my lord, that you are not?"

"No," said Tagh heavily. "I can't say that." He groped for a chair, a man suddenly very old and feeling the weight of his years. Dully he said, "There are two things we haven't told you. One is that the ship from Kotan was commanded by my son."

"And the other?"

"My world is in peril."

Chalom stepped to the table and slammed his hand on the unrolled chart.

"Look," he commanded. "Never mind the formulae, look at the path I have plotted. Here is Krait, there Natush, there Gromol, and here," his finger lifted to point, "here is Kotan. I have plotted the region a dozen times and checked my calculations a hundred. There is no room for doubt. Kotan lies in the path of the Omphalos. It is moving towards it, carried by the galactic drift. Unless something can prevent it the

27

entire planet will follow the exploratory ships into oblivion. Now do you understand why we must keep trying?"

"You," said Carodyne. "Not me. My lord, just what is it you want me to do?"

It was late when he left the Ekal, the lodge settled for the night, but not all were asleep. Carodyne sensed her presence the moment he entered his room. She stood before the window looking at the night beyond, very tall, dressed all in black, gems set in her hair, sparkling as she turned so that, for a moment, she seemed crowned in living fire. Then she was against him, pressing close, the scent of her perfume filling his nostrils.

"Mark! How could you have left me?"

Quietly he said, "You don't have to do this, Shara. It isn't necessary."

Startled she stepped back. "You know?"

"It was obvious. You asked too many questions and you knew Nev Chalom. It was careless of you to have mentioned him. Were you trying to arouse my curiosity a little? Paving the way for what you knew was to come?"

"So it's in the open," she said. "And you may not believe it but I'm glad. I'm working with the Ekal and I admit it. It started as a job in which I had a personal interest, but now it's a little more than that. I wasn't acting just then, trying to snare you with my body so you would be amenable to suggestion. That was for real." She paused and, when he made no comment, said, "All right, now you know how I feel about you. If you want to throw me out go right ahead, but before you do I'd like to know one thing. Did you accept the Ekal's proposition?"

"I'm a gambler," he said flatly. "Not a candidate for suicide. You know what Tagh Altin intends. He wants to investigate the Omphalos and he wants me to help him do it. Seven recorded failures to date and still he wants to try again. He must be obsessed."

"No," she corrected. "Desperate. He came to Krait looking for a certain type of man and he found him—you. He isn't sending anyone to his death. If Chalom didn't explain he should have done. The ship isn't going into the Omphalos. It's going to remain close to the edge. There is a point close to the barrier where the energies must intermingle. A trained man could guide a small probe close to it, follow it and take measurements from which something could be learned. Who better to act as a pilot than a skimmer? But you know all this. They must have explained."

"They did."

"Then?"

"Coincidence," he said, "It works both ways." A bottle stood on a small table and he lifted it, pouring out two drinks. Handing her one he said, "Let's drink to coincidence."

"Why not?" She sipped at her brandy. "Are you taking the job?"

"I'm thinking about it."

"Why the hesitation? Didn't he offer enough money?"

"I'm risking my life. How much do you think it's worth?"

"Do you want me to persuade him to increase his offer?" She looked at him for a long moment, then added, "I'll do it if it's what you want, but I don't think you do. This talk of money is just a facade, a skin you're wearing to protect something you regard as soft. Maybe you were hurt when young, trusted someone too much, or followed someone who let you down. My brother—he did that once. Trusted and got hurt and then appeared to be hard. But it was all on the surface."

"Tell me about him."

"My brother?" She lifted her glass and looked at the spirits it contained, the deep gold warm against the crystal, the softness of her skin. "My brother," she said, and emptied the glass.

"Dead?"

"Gone. Does it matter?"

"It matters. Especially if he was on one of the ships which got lost. Was it the last? The one with the telepath on board?"

"Damn you," she said without heat. "You know too much and read people too well. How did you guess?"

"You told me that you had a personal interest in working for the Ekal. Elgesh isn't anywhere near Kotan and so his problem isn't yours. You're anxious to help investigate the Omphalos and you drank a toast to the departed. You're young so he couldn't have been very old. Therefore he had to be on the last ship." He refilled her glass. "And that is

29

why you left your home world, not to hunt up a husband, but to try and find your brother. You shouldn't waste your time."

"It's my time."

"And your life," he agreed. "Let us drink to it. A long one and happy all the way." He paused and added, softly. "And let the dead bury the dead."

Advice from a professional, she thought, looking at him. And she had been wrong about the inner softness. There was nothing weak or soft about him, gentleness, perhaps, but that was all. A hard man, ruthless, who would let nothing stand in his way.

With sudden insight she said, "You maneuvered this. You wanted to meet the Ekal, to gain his confidence and to be offered a job. Did you know what he intended?"

"He has a ship on the field and a crew too fond of talking."

"Coincidence," she said. "That's why you drank to it. You were looking for a man like the Ekal and he was looking for a man like you. You will help him?"

"Of course."

"You could have told me that when first I asked. Damn you, Mark! Were you trying to win confidences or get your revenge? Well, it doesn't matter, not now. You've told me all I want to know. Almost all."

"Shara, you are a very beautiful woman."

"Thank you, Mark. That's what I've been waiting to hear."

4

AT a distance the Omphalos was a sigil, closer and it was a mystery, closer still and it resembled an endless sea. The surface which seemed to be smooth, silken, held the restless movement of an ocean. There were ripples, swells, gigantic waves which rose, threatening at any moment to engulf the tiny craft in which he rode. And the colors were blinding.

Carodyne lifted his visor and rubbed at his burning eyes as the drive lifted him away from the luminescent danger. He was sweating, his muscles jumping with the strain of tension too long maintained, his body an ache of unremitting effort. From the radio came Chalom's voice, sharp, irritating.

"We need another run, Mark. Closer this time if you can make it."

Carodyne ignored the voice.

"Mark? Come in if you can hear me. Mark?"

"I can hear you and the answer is no."

"What do you mean? I've got to check the readings and on that last run you made the instruments seem to go all to hell."

"Why don't you follow them?"

For a moment there was silence and then, less harsh, the voice said, "I know it isn't easy, Mark, but it's important. Unless I can make one more check the results will be invalid. We need one more run to finalize this series. I think I'm on to something but I have to be sure."

"All right," said Carodyne. "Give me a little time."

He leaned back in the seat, forcing himself to relax, taking deep breaths and looking at the top of the cramped cockpit. It was bare metal, without interest, but anything was better than looking at the Omphalos. It was too big. Suns could be swallowed up in it, entire solar systems, planets without number. Against it he felt like an ant on a mountain. And, worse than the size, the grandeur, was the mystery it contained.

The metal at which he stared shone red, then green, then a vivid blue. Gas, he thought, great clouds of it swirling, moved by conflicting forces, radiating in a variety of flu-

31

orescent colors. A facile, comforting explanation, but no one knew if it was true. No one could know with the barrier preventing any true investigation.

"Mark?"

"Not yet."

The ship in which he sat was built like a skimmer, a tiny cockpit, the body crammed with the drive mechanism and a load of instruments. Others hung outside the hull, a fringe of metal spikes, plates, a scoop, assorted grids of various alloys. Chalom's toys, the things with which he hoped to win a secret which so far had defied investigation.

Carodyne felt himself ease a little and dropped his eyes to the instrument panel, the things on which his life depended. All read as they should but the most important tool of all was the one he could not see. The brain housed in his body, the organic mechanism which governed his every action. Himself.

Lowering his visor he studied the enemy.

It was easy to think of it as that. It had taken life, swallowing it without a trace; it threatened his own existence, and anything which did that was automatically an enemy. The size didn't matter, the mystery, the mind-wrenching splendor. It could kill and therefore was dangerous and had to be treated with respect. Only the dead underestimated their enemies—the living knew better.

And, like a living thing, the Omphalos had a skin.

It was a band of about a mile in depth, minute when compared to the overall size, a region in which normal space seemed to meet something utterly strange, to mingle with it and to be converted. Beyond it matter simply vanished. Within it, possibly, it was changed. Outside it lay safety. Chalom wanted his instruments to dangle within it, to test and measure and send back their findings to the parent ship.

"Mark?"

"Ready now," said Carodyne. He took a final deep breath. "Heading in."

He should have kept talking, maintained a running commentary, but after the first minute of the first run he had refused. Talk needed a little concentration, not too much but more than he was willing to spare. Skimming the Omphalos

32

demanded total output of mind and body, a situation in which babble had no place.

Gently he adjusted the controls and fell slowly towards the surface of the luminous sea.

And, as always, images began to cloud his brain.

A field thick with ripening corn, a woman, a small house and the shapes of children. A river in which fish sported with finny abandon. A crystal glowing with radiance, strings of dancing words, skeins of musical notes, a somber shadow immediately replaced by an open door framing a landscape bright with flowers and sunlight.

He ignored them, concentrating, feeling the tension beginning to mount, the tremors of arms and legs, the knotted muscle at the back of his neck. Lower, lower to where a patch of azure swam in a ring of emerald. Up quickly to avoid a lance of ruby, higher as a curl of purple moved towards him, down again as he followed the convolutions of the mass below.

A tiny mote following the line between wind and water on the surface of a storm-ridden sea.

A hand lifted towards him, delicate, with nails of gleaming diamond, the fingers long, beckoning. It fell away and an eye, slanted, without iris or pupil, winked with subtle lechery. A face, snarling, mouth filled with crimson teeth, flaring nostrils shining blue dissolved into charred and steaming ruin. Fragments of a thousand distorted scenes, barely remembered, assembled by the interplay of light and the impact of invisible energies. And, with it, came the hunger, the feral need for sustenance, the Omphalos crying to be fed.

The enemy waiting to spring.

The concept saved him. Eyes burning, Carodyne eased back on the controls, lifting the fragile craft high above the swirling mass of color with its hypnotic attraction. His hands trembled as he sent the vessel heading into space and spoke into the radio.

"Chalom?"

"Yes, Mark."

"I'm coming in."

"But, Mark! That run was short. I need more data and—"

Carodyne snarled his anger. "Damn your data! I'm coming in!"

33

Shara met him as he left the dock. She wore a single garment of close-fitting material tight to legs and arms, snug about the body, a feminine version of the tough coverall spacemen wore. Her hair was bound and crested over her head. As she saw him her eyes widened.

"Mark! Are you all right?"

He caught a glimpse of his face in a polished bulkhead. The skin was tight over his bones, his bloodshot eyes edged with sooted rings.

"I'll live."

"You'd better." She took his arm as he moved through the vessel. It was a freighter, the hold converted to hold the tiny investigating craft, the monitoring instruments. Carodyne heard the captain's voice as they neared the door.

"My lord, with respect, the terms of the charter are plain. To coast beside the Omphalos at a safe distance. This we have done and are doing."

The Ekal's voice rose dry and pointed.

"And who, captain, decides a safe distance?"

"I do, my lord."

"Then, captain, it appears there is no argument. That will be all."

The door opened and the captain emerged. He was a short, stocky man with a peculiarly elongated face and a skull which rose in a pronounced peak between his ears. A product of the Tern system, normally phlegmatic and unemotional. He glanced at Carodyne and shook his head.

"Man, you look terrible."

"I feel it. Trouble?"

"A difference of opinion." He bowed to the girl. "With your leave, madam? Sir?"

Chalom sat with the Ekal. His hair was wilder than normal, strands lifted by his raking fingers standing like spikes over his head. He was furious.

"You should have been stronger with him, my lord. The ship is standing too far out. We could halve the distance and still ride in perfect safety."

"He is the captain," said Tagh quietly. "On Kotan I rule. Here, on this ship, he is master."

"We should have built a vessel of our own. A special ship

34

designed for a special purpose. One with facilities we do not have. I asked for it, my lord. I begged for it. Now we have to suffer the whims of a coward." He turned and saw Carodyne and the girl. "You, Mark. I thought that at least I could rely on you. Why did you cut short the run?"

"Look at him," she said. "There's your answer."

"Mark?"

"Damn it," she stormed. "Can't you see he's exhausted? Do you think it easy to go out there and risk your life every second of the time?"

"So he's tired," snapped Chalom. "So we're all tired. I haven't slept more than a few hours since we left Krait. But there's work to be done and we won't do it standing around. Maybe," he said spitefully, "if you left him alone, he wouldn't be so fatigued."

For a moment she froze and then, stepping forward, lifted her hand to strike. Carodyne caught her wrist before the blow could land.

To Chalom he said, "Apologize."

"To her?"

"To us both. To her for your insinuation, to me for implying that I am falling down on the job. Do it!"

From where he sat the Ekal said, dryly, "I should obey, Chalom. You will probably have cause to regret it if you don't."

For a moment he hesitated, stubborn, too blinded by his single-minded purpose to have thought for the concern of others. Then he shrugged. "All right," he said. "I'm sorry. But, damn it, there is so much to do. When will you be ready to make another run, Mark?"

"Why?"

"For more data, of course, what else. I need more measurements and I want to try some new alloys on the grids."

"For even more measurements?"

"Of course."

"Why?"

Chalom stared blankly at the question then shook his head. "I don't understand, Mark. Isn't it obvious?"

"The only thing obvious is that you want to send me out there until I die," said Carodyne harshly. "I've done eleven runs, one more than we agreed was necessary. And still you aren't satisfied. You never will be. If you can't make sense out of the data you already have then more will be useless. If you want to take more measurements then go out there and get them yourself. I'm finished."

"Another one?" Chalom didn't bother to hide his sneer. "First the captain and now you. A fine pair you make."

"You called the captain a coward," said Carodyne tightly. "Are you applying that word to me?"

"You know the old saying. If the cap fits—" He broke off as fingers closed around his throat. They felt like claws of steel.

"Listen," said Carodyne. "You called me a coward, now I'm going to call you something. A parasite. You know what that is? Vermin which lives on others. For years you've wanted the chance to investigate the Omphalos—or so you claimed. You've lived on the Ekal's money and fed him with promises. Now, when you can't deliver the goods you promised, you whine for more data. You don't want more data, you want an excuse to hang on, to sponge, to live high and rich. You want an excuse to fail." His hand tightened a little. "Or perhaps an excuse to die. Some men consider it to be a form of escape."

"You're mad!" croaked Chalom. "Insane!"

It could be true. Carodyne released the throat, stepping back, feeling the pulse of berserk rage. His temples throbbed as he fought for control. The Omphalos, he thought. That thing out there, watching, waiting, playing tricks with the mind. Probing strengths and accompanying weaknesses. Feeding on them, perhaps?

He wondered at the thought.

The Ekal said, "We have more data than you knew, Chalom. Obviously close proximity of the Omphalos causes mental aberration. A change of some kind, certainly an alteration in personality. Or perhaps it is a release of the true nature of man." He paused, musing. "A kaleidoscope," he murmured. "Could a brain be composed of many patterns each triggered into dominance by the correct stimulus? As we see images in the light could a man see his other natures? False ones, perhaps, as the images are false?"

"That belongs to the realm of philosophy, my lord," said Chalom rubbing his throat. "I am a scientist."

"And is not philosophy a science? Some have called it a mirror in which to see truth." He was ironic, a little goading. "But no matter. Presh, some refreshment."

He stepped forward from Carodyne's side where he had appeared at the first sign of violence, silently filling glasses and handing them around. Carodyne swallowed the liquid at a gulp, Chalom sputtering as he tasted the brandy.

Shara said, "Have you learned anything, Nev?"

"To guard my tongue, perhaps," he said wryly. "But aside from that very little. I think that it might be possible to penetrate the Omphalos if certain precautions are taken. As far as I can discover there is an actual transmutation, a transition, rather, from our space to whatever lies within. I lack data, of course," he added with a sharp look at Carodyne, "so it is impossible to be precise. And there is also the question of temporal displacement."

A cloud of words meaning nothing. He realized it and made an attempt to be more meaningful.

"I must speak in analogy. Imagine two spaces separated by a sheet of water. On one side the space is very cold, on the other very hot. Imagine too that the water is an almost perfect nonconductor. Now, if a mote hit the water from the cold side it would be relatively unaffected by the molecular motion, but, as it penetrated deeper, it would be thrown about. The closer it got to the hot side the greater the motion. From the viewpoint of those watching from the cold side it would simply vanish. They would be static, the mote would suddenly acquire tremendous velocity. It would dart off at a speed too great to follow."

"And the temporal displacement?"

"I don't know, Shara," he confessed. "I'm guessing, a thing no scientist should ever do. But follow the analogy and you will see what I mean. Our mote could, if all things were equal, still communicate. It would be somewhere distant, moving at an incredible speed in relation to its monitoring vessel, but, feasibly, its signals could be received. But if it were in a region where time moved a thousand times as fast? Or a thousand times as slow? You see the problem?"

Carodyne said, "Have you evidence of that?"

"A hint, no more."

"And the precautions you spoke of?"

"If we could build a ship with special mechanisms to heterodyne the energy levels, one that could actually vary its space-time references, then we could, possibly, enter the Omphalos and return. That is assuming my theories are correct. Aside from that?" He shrugged and turned to the Ekal. "I am sorry, my lord, but it would be dishonest to offer a hope I do not possess."

"You have given me hope," said the Ekal. "Hope that my son could have lived, could still be living. The others too."

And the hope, unspoken, that even if Kotan should be swallowed by the Omphalos the population need not die.

Carodyne drank the last of his brandy. "And your other theory? The pulse?"

"That has not changed." He added, acidly, not forgetting the soreness of his throat, "Perhaps, because you have studied the Omphalos so closely, you could add a few comments of your own?"

"A pulse is an expansion followed by a contraction. How do we know what period of the cycle the Omphalos is in? It could already be contracting, that it is as large now as it will ever be. It could get much smaller in the course of time. So small that Kotan would be in no danger."

"Holman's rule of stars—"

"Could be wrong."

Chalom was sarcastic. "Naturally you speak as a qualified astrophysicist who has an alternate theory to account for the missing worlds. If so I would be happy to hear it."

"I'm not a scientist," said Carodyne, rising. "But one thing I do know, a scientist is not God, and only God can never be wrong."

Outside the room he leaned against a bulkhead, feeling the coolness of the metal against his forehead. He felt weak, drained, the stimulus of the brandy fading as he walked down the passage towards his cabin. As he reached it the captain came towards him.

"Something unusual has occurred," he said. "I would like your opinion on what is best to do."

38

"You are the master of the ship, captain."

"This has nothing to do with my vessel. The Omphalos—if you will please come to the observation room?"

Incredibly it had changed. The swirling mass of light showed an ebon blotch, ragged, ugly, harsh against the glowing colors.

"I have never seen this before," said the captain. "My contract calls for me to remain a safe distance—but am I justified in moving further out? The Ekal has great influence and power and I would not like to be the victim of a complaint."

Carodyne said, "Summon the others. Quickly!"

He heard them arrive, the sharp intake of Chalom's breath, the grip of Shara's fingers on his arm.

"Mark! What's happening?"

"A thing we could wait for a lifetime to happen and never see again." Chalom quivered with eagerness. "Don't you see? A break in the pattern. That blotch can only be a rupture of some kind. It must be examined, measurements made, data collected. Mark!"

He remained silent, looking at the blotch, thinking of the turbulence which must cover the area, his own fatigue.

The Ekal spoke, his voice a dry rustle in the control room. "I ask for my world, Mark. For Kotan. Double what you have already earned if you will do one more run."

"Can he refuse?" Chalom looked baffled. "The chance of a lifetime to learn something about the Omphalos. A freak event which could tell us everything we want to know. For God's sake, man, don't just stand there. Get ready to go!"

And Shara, her arm soft, her fingers quivering.

"Please, Mark! Please!"

A fool, he thought, as he moved the tiny craft from the converted freighter. A man doing what he knew was beyond his capacity, yet doing it just the same. Driven by what? Not money, not the urging of Chalom and not even that of the girl. By curiosity. By the desire to know. The need to kill, in a sense, the enemy which the Omphalos had become.

To learn its secret and render it harmless as man had once done to fire, to the lightning, to space itself. To understand and, by understanding, to control.

They watched him as he went, Chalom busy with his instruments, the rest looking at the monitor screen which showed the gaping orifice, the tiny vessel vanishing to reappear, crossing, dipping, climbing over the ebon patch.

"So close," Shara whispered. "He's so very close."

"The readings!" Chalom was jubilant, fired with the enthusiasm of the scientist against which nothing held more importance than the gathering of knowledge. "The things I can learn!"

The Ekal remained silent, watching, his face creased and his eyes softer than usual. Thinking of his son, his world, perhaps even of the man in the tiny vessel far away. Watching as the ebon blotch writhed, twisted into the shape of a hungry mouth and then, like a mouth, snapped shut.

Chalom said, blankly, "He's gone. The instruments aren't recording. He's gone."

"Dead," said Shara dully. "We forced him to go. We killed him. Mark!"

She felt the weight of the Ekal's hand on her shoulder, thin, dry, the touch of a leaf.

"Go to your cabin, my dear," he said gently. "You also, Chalom."

"But, my lord, there is work to be done."

"Tomorrow will suffice. Go."

Alone the Ekal sat and looked at his board. The pieces winked back at him, red and green, bright colors set on gold and silver. He picked up one, a pawn, and sat looking at it for a long time. And then, with sudden anger, threw it hard against the wall.

5

CARODYNE was not dead, not dreaming, but mad. Insane in the sense that he was lost in a world of delusion which was totally unreal. A part of his mind knew that he was in a ship and had penetrated into the Omphalos, but it was a dwindling part and the fact was already becoming vague. The rest was nightmare.

Reality is the impressions received by the sensory apparatus of the body transmitted to and interpreted by the brain. But it is a two-way traffic; the brain can make its own reality restricted only by natural law. And, in the Omphalos, natural law did not apply.

Carodyne screamed as he was bathed in fire, seared by acids, torn by savage forces. Images replaced the hard contours of the cockpit, gibbering faces, drooling mouths, a plethora of creatures spawned in the deepest depths of delirium. The world expanded, became clouds of gas, giant crystals, endless plains covered with scudding wisps of white, red and green. He plunged through a forest of bones, drowned in turgid seas, sank into quicksands. His mind, responding to strange energies, built endless fantasies as it tried to force the unknown rush of stimuli into recognizable patterns. Tried and failed and tried again as Carodyne writhed in anguish.

Desperately he tried to channel his thoughts and cling to a fragment of what he thought was the truth. I'm Mark Carodyne and I'm in a ship trapped in the Omphalos. Mark Carodyne in a ship trapped in the Omphalos. Mark Carodyne in a ship trapped in the Omphalos.

It was too much, something had to go.

Mark Carodyne in a ship. Mark Carodyne in a ship. Mark Carodyne, Mark Carodyne, Carodyne, Carodyne, Carodyne...

His name, his identity, the only thing now he could be sure of. The Omphalos was a word, the ship a dream, the fragment of a recent nightmare, but still, stubbornly, he clung to it, remembering the ebon blotch, the sickening moment when he had known that he had ventured a little too far, risked too much, had gambled and had lost.

No wonder the mate of the telepath had gone insane, that commentaries had broken off in mid-word. And the radios and other instruments? What instruments? Here they did not exist. His ship did not exist. Nothing was real aside from his name, his ego, the self which refused to yield.

I'm dead, he thought, dissolved, scattered in a cloud of atoms to brighten the flaring colors. I've a million eyes and can see in all directions. I'm omnipotent and eternal.

But that too was a part of the delusion.

Carodyne, he thought desperately. A man. In a ship—what was a ship? In the Omphalos—what was the Omphalos? Carodyne. A man. Carodyne. Carodyne.

Old enemies came and he shot them down. The slope stretched before him and he flew down it like a bird. A woman reached for him and he felt the warmth of soft arms, the pressure of soft flesh. It changed. Everything changed. Strange shapes danced past on articulated limbs, pyramids hung against a yellow sky, balls of ruby shattered to release pulsating blobs of luminous jelly, he ran down an endless rope, was stretched, squeezed, stroked, pummeled, drenched in perfume and covered with filth. His ears rang with bells, gongs, chimes, brazen clangings, a thousand notes, discords, harmonies. Taste, sight, sound, smell and feeling, all were mixed in a wild confusion. Madness. There could be only one escape.

In the darkness he heard voices.

"Unusual, sister, you agree?"

"Indeed yes, brother."

"A hard one, stubborn, good sport for our game."

"My piece, brother."

"You move too fast. Let us savor the moment and then, perhaps, come to a compromise. Such determination must not be spoiled."

"So rare, brother, so very rare."

"And to be used with discretion. An opportunity not to be other than relished and used with discernment. And mine, I think."

"Mine, brother."

42

"You are hard, sister."

"But determined."

"Sister?"

"Brother!"

The soft sound of amusement tinged with undertones of iron resolve.

Carodyne stirred and opened his eyes. He hadn't been asleep, not even unconscious in the true sense of the word; his brain had protected itself against the raging flood of stimuli by blacking out as eyes will become temporarily blind after being exposed to light too intense. A refuge against insanity.

Yet what he saw was impossible by all familiar terms of reference.

He stood on a rolling plain covered with scudding banks of cloud beneath a sky banded as a rainbow with colors sharply defined. In the air hung geometrical shapes slowly turning, changing as they turned, cones into spheres into cubes into tetrahedrons. Rods, spirals, curves which writhed and swelled to become strings of globules, clustered eggs, loops and tangles of endless tubes. Far in the distance monstrous shapes loomed against the rainbow sky. Mountains? Banks of cloud? Mirages distorted from regions unguessed? He couldn't tell.

He looked down at his hands and clenched them, feeling the pressure of his nails against his palms. That, at least, was real, or had he only imagined the clenching, the pressure? He closed his eyes and tried again, imagining a confined space, metal, dials of transparent material behind which needles swung. The picture disturbed him with familiar associations, a ship, an ebon blotch, pain and terror. A best forgotten nightmare.

He looked again at the plain, the geometrical shapes, the impossible sky.

Illusion, he thought. A reality I am unable to comprehend. A four-dimensional region which I am trying to understand with three-dimensional senses. More than four, perhaps, but alien to everything I know.

The plain changed. The ground became soft, covered with grass and delicate flowers. The banks of moving cloud solidified into bushes and trees. The only familiar things he knew which could hang suspended in the air were birds or artifacts and artifacts did not change their shape. A turning cone became an eagle, a twisted mass of looping tubes a flight of starlings, other shapes became clouds fleeced against the sky of golden shimmers. A reality determined by the necessity of his brain to understand. Illusion, still, perhaps, but one which he could comprehend.

Only the distant shapes remained vague, ominous in some way, disturbing.

He began to walk towards them. To either side the bushes passed, the trees, while overhead the birds wheeled and made thin sounds as if calling or warning of his coming. And, as he walked, he seemed to dream so that he seemed withdrawn, set in a place apart and watching a man walk across a plain towards gigantic shapes which dwindled as he approached and became two auras of glowing light which rested on the rim of a wide amphitheater filled with some mysterious device.

A dream which ended as he halted and looked at what lay before him.

A lattice of countless open cubes each filled with a multitude of pieces blurred and defying recognition. The shapes of glowing light which had once been mountains and which now, even as he watched, shrank and changed.

"Shara!"

She stood before him, smiling, the crested ebon of her hair glinting with gems, the curves of her body taut against cloth of gold. And then he looked again and knew it wasn't the girl, that it couldn't be her, that it was a familiar, comforting shape he had placed on something else.

And the other?

Chalom with his bitter mouth and snapping eyes and hair in wild disarray. But the picture was wrong, somehow it didn't fit, and it changed as he watched, became smaller, older, the face narrowing and the eyes becoming shrewd. The Ekal, Tagh Altin sitting before his board as he had done so often.

His board?

The colossal lattice too had changed, diminished by his

need to understand. Now it was flat and composed of a thousand squares thronged with castles and towers, cities and towns, small pieces and large and a variety of colors. A world, a universe in miniature, the symbols manipulated in a game played by what? Not a man and woman, of that he was sure. The shapes they wore were illusion and they were opposed, male and female, light and darkness, positive and negative. And between them, he sensed, lay conflict, thinly disguised but unmistakable.

He said, "My name is Carodyne. Mark Carodyne."

"We know." Her voice was like one he vaguely remembered, warm, soft, seeming to hold the chime of bells. Had Shara owned such a voice?

He said, harshly, "I do not understand how I came to be here. I was in a ship—something happened. How did I escape?"

"Familiar associations are beginning to restore mental stability," said the man. His voice too was like that of the Ekal. Dry, calculating, a mask for thoughts. And yet both held another familiarity. They were the voices he had heard while in darkness.

"Conflict, brother?"

"Inevitable, sister. Adjustments will have to be made."

"On so rare a piece?"

"We have no choice."

"Agreed, brother, but with care. I shall attend to it."

"You, sister?"

"The piece is mine."

"That has yet to be decided."

Carodyne stirred, impatient, feeling his anger rise at the argument. He was a man, not a thing to be disposed of at a whim. And he sensed they ere talking about himself.

"I don't know what you're talking about," he snapped. "But if you have an argument settle it the easy way. With a coin."

The woman smiled. "You have one?"

He found a decal and poised the heavy disc of metal. On one side was a serpent, on the other an egg. "The serpent is male, the egg female. Agreed?"

"Spin," said the man. He seemed amused. He watched as

45

the coin flashed, settled on the ground. "You win, sister. Shall we commence?"

"A moment. The rules?"

"As always. He lives or he dies."

"No more?" She paused as if thinking. "I think there should be a little more. A refinement, perhaps, and one of interest to all concerned. I suggest—"

"Wait!" Carodyne stared at them, at the board, the assembled pieces. "I want to know what you are doing, what all this is about. I'm a man, not a thing to be used as a token in a game. I don't belong here."

"That is immaterial. Sister?"

"A prize," she said. "A reward. Mark, what is it you most desire?"

"To be free."

"Then find yourself—when you do freedom will be yours. And now, brother, commence!"

The shapes were already vague, the human lineaments fading, dissolving into blurs of light. Something like a hand reached towards the board. A piece was lifted, moved, set down in another place.

And, for Carodyne, the world changed.

6

HE was on a horse riding in a blizzard, dressed in garments which were strange. Thick gauntlets, high boots, leather trousers, a brigandine which covered his body from throat to thigh with metal scales. A helmet, a high-collared cloak, a wide belt from which hung a sheathed sword and dagger.

An armed and armored horseman riding alone in a storm.

Carodyne made no attempt to question what he saw. The horse was real, the wind, the snow, the forest through which he rode, the trees stretching to either side, ghostly in the dying light. And he was real. He could feel the numbing cold, the saddle between his thighs, the weight of the cloak. He was a man who had ridden hard and far and was hopelessly lost.

Lost?

Transposed, rather. He remembered the ship, the closing darkness of the ebon patch as the Omphalos had swallowed him, the strange plain and the golden shapes. Somehow he must have landed in his madness and wandered and reached the place where they had played their game. And then?

A piece, manipulated, moved, given clothes and a mount and set like an actor on a stage—to do what?

Find himself, the woman had said. Find himself and be free.

Later he would think about it.

The horse stumbled, quivering a little as Carodyne leaned forward. He touched the neck with a soothing hand, feeling the bunch of powerful muscles, and pressure against the reins. Years ago he had learned to ride and to practice martial arts, skills he had never forgotten. Then they had been used

47

in make-believe games of war, historical reconstructions set in the rolling parks of Earth. Now, perhaps, they could serve a grimmer purpose.

He drew the sword from its scabbard. The hilt was of some metal like brass, leather-bound, studded and ridged to ensure a firm grip. The guard was a downcurving crosspiece, the pommel a massive knob. The blade was thirty inches long, straight, double-edged, razor sharp and viciously pointed. The dagger was a shorter version of the sword.

Not toys, but real, things holding within themselves the beauty of functional purpose. Instruments designed to stab, to slash, to cut and to kill.

The wind caught his ears as he removed the helmet, whining, chilling his uncovered scalp, piling thickly on his hair. The helmet was padded, shaped to cover back and sides, rising low to his eyes and the nape of his neck. A slotted visor could be dropped to cover the face.

Thoughtfully he replaced it, thankful, at least, that he hadn't been thrown naked into this strange environment. Without protection he would have frozen, foundering in the snow piled thickly all around, his body heat lost beneath the impact of the freezing wind. But he had arms, clothes and a stallion on which to ride.

To where?

Carodyne scowled as he rode before the wind, feeling the snow pile against his back, mounding on his shoulders and dragging at his cloak. There was too much snow. It filled the air, swirling, ghostly in the dying light. It covered the ground with a featureless blanket, piling on leaves and branches so that even the trees lost their identity and became a formless blur. Among them lurked danger.

He heard the sound above the gusting wind, thin, menacing, rising to be echoed from a point ahead. Beneath him the horse snorted and began to quiver.

"Steady!"

Carodyne's left hand was firm on the reins as he soothed the animal with his right. Wolves were to be expected in a forest. The storm would have driven them from their lairs, starving, eager to make a kill. They would have scented both horse and rider and now be closing in.

He narrowed his eyes, cursing the snow, the inability to see more than a little way ahead. Night was falling and soon it would be dark. Unless he could find shelter soon, neither he or the stallion would live to see the dawn.

He touched spurs to the heaving flanks. The howling came again, closer, the sound a sharper goad than those on his heels. The stallion loped forward, the thud of the hooves becoming a monotonous accompaniment to the wind. The lope became a gallop as Carodyne guided the animal between the trees, following what he hoped was a winding path. It opened as they crossed a small clearing, turning to climb a gradient, and, as they reached the crest, he saw a glimmer of light.

It came from a beacon set on a tower which rose high above gabled roofs. It threw a dancing glow on the snow, the shuttered windows and blank walls of a sprawling building. A gate opened as he approached, spilling a flood of light into the gloom. Men armed with crossbows watched as he dismounted and led the stallion into a low-roofed area with a stone floor. It stank of sweat, manure, leather and urine, the normal scents of any stable, but there were others, just as identifying. The place was an inn.

"Welcome, stranger." A big, full-bodied man came forward as the guards slammed shut the gate. He wore a stained leather apron over a tunic of brown edged with yellow. In the light of cressets his face was ruddy, smiling. "I am Deltmar. This hostelry is mine. Your name, friend?"

"Mark Carodyne."

"Of?" Deltmar shrugged as Carodyne made no answer. "Well, each man's business is his own and I question none as long as he can settle his reckoning." He glanced at the stallion. The beast's head was low, his flanks heaving. "You have ridden him hard. The beasts?"

"Yes."

"They were close?"

"Too close," said Carodyne grimly. "If I hadn't seen your light they would be feasting now."

"We do what we can," said Deltmar. "Always at night the beacon is lit, during the day also at times of storm. A guide for travelers seeking a safe refuge. But the wolves are bad this year. Game is scarce and the winter drags. Well, we can

49

take care of your mount. A bucket of mulled ale laced with poppy juice, hot blankets and a double measure of grain will restore his strength. And for yourself? A private chamber, perhaps; one so lordly will not care to share. A cup of hot wine to take the chill from your bones?" He clapped his hands as Carodyne nodded. "Arota! Attend our guest!"

A stripling appeared and led Carodyne up a flight of stairs to a small room, barely furnished and chill despite the fire which burned in a grate made of slabs of stone. He vanished to reappear with a leathern cup filled with hot, spiced wine, watching as Carodyne drank.

"If you will give me your cloak, master, I will see that it is dried." He took the sopping fabric. "Is there anything else you require?"

"A bath," said Carodyne.

"A bath, master? In this weather?"

He sensed the boy's incredulity. "Some hot water then. In a bucket. With soap and a towel." He held out the empty cup. "Before you get it fetch me some more wine."

Alone, he stripped and washed. Beneath the brigandine he'd worn a thin tunic of supple leather, the skin of a lizard of some kind, finely scaled and bright with natural color. And, around his neck, he found a golden chain.

He examined it with interest. It was crudely made, the links roughly hammered, pressed close but unjoined. They could be opened and removed without trouble, more added in case of need. A neat and easy way to carry wealth for a man who traveled in a world probably devoid of banks and credit systems.

He dressed to go below, donning only the tunic, pants and high boots. The chain he refastened around his neck, hesitating over the weapon belt and finally lifting the sword from its housing and taking only the dagger. It might be the custom to bear arms in the communal room or it might not. The dagger would be a safe compromise. At the foot of the stairs he passed a girl bearing a tray of smoking meat. Their eyes met and he suffered a shock of recognition. Shara? He looked again; she was just a girl with black hair and bold eyes who smiled an invitation.

"Is there anything I could give you, master? No? Well, the

50

night is young. My name is Wilma if you should change your mind."

Carodyne smiled and passed her to enter the room.

It was long, low, dark wood gleaming in the light of fires, lanterns and flambeaux set in iron sockets and backed by sheets of polished copper. A gallery ran around it leading to the upper chambers. Before one of the fires an animal roasted on a spit turned by a system of falling weights. The floor and furniture were of wood stained and polished by use and time. Trophies hung on the walls, antlered heads, the masks of wolves, tusks of boars sprouting from frozen snarls.

A warm place, snug, filled with pleasant odors. A good place to be while the storm raged outside.

Carodyne sat at the table and ate meat and bread crusted with seeds. Replete he leaned back, nursing a tankard of ale, looking at the rest of the company. They were what he'd expected to find. Some merchants sitting close at a communal board, each trying to outboast the other with talk of fat profits and rare merchandise. Their guards, a cluster of men and boys, boisterous as they reached for the serving girls. A pair of traveling musicians making soft noises with flute and drum. A score of men filling the air with the soft drone of talk.

To one side a man sat at a table accompanied by a handful of youths. He wore a robe of yellow held by a crimson sash. His black hair was piled in a knot above his head and his face, sere and bland, held the texture of weathered parchment. A bowl stood before him into which he probed with a pointed stick, spearing and popping fragments of food into his lipless mouth. A wandering philosopher, those who listened either his pupils or strangers eager to learn. As he ate he talked, his voice thin, penetrating.

"And there are those who hold to the belief that we live in hell, that this world is a place of punishment to which we are sent to expiate crimes done in some other existence. Maybe so, who can tell the Master Plan? Yet I do not think this is the case. I believe that we each of us holds within ourselves the elements of both pain and pleasure. That we

51

each make our own misery and our own joy and we do it in the manner in which we regard the world."

"Master?" One of the youths frowned. "Would you clarify? I fear that I do not understand."

The philosopher dug into his bowl and looked thoughtfully at a segment of chopped worm wriggling on the end of his stick. He chewed, swallowed, looked at another of the youths.

"You, Geyouk. Explain."

The youth swelled with self-importance. "A man who has nothing can be miserable or joyful. Miserable because he lacks what others possess or joyful because he has nothing to lose. A man with one leg can be happy that he has not lost both. A woman, dying young, can be thankful she has been spared the tribulations of age. Always, if you seek it, there is reason for thankfulness and joy."

The philosopher nodded, stirring the contents of his bowl. "There you have it," he said. "The summation of existence. All is transitory and nothing is worth the pain of fear or envy. All end the same. We are born, we live, we die. Why then turn these brief years into a self-made torment? Hell is for those who seek it. Heaven is a point of view."

One of the students frowned. "But, master," he protested. "That is the philosophy of a slave. Is man just an animal to be content with so little? Have you no means to ensure joy for all?"

"Means? No. A rule, yes." Again the pointed stick speared a juicy morsel. "True happiness can only be achieved in one way. It is this—let not your reach extend beyond your grasp."

"Master?"

"If you cannot acquire more of the fruits of the world then desire less," said the philosopher patiently. "Why yearn for what you cannot obtain? Is it not more simple to cease from yearning?"

Geyouk said, "But, master, that is to negate all ambition. If men had not yearned to remain warm they would never have learned to control fire. If our host did not seek to improve his position by selling us food and shelter then we would now be crouching in the snow. If all ceased from striving, what then?"

"The answer to that depends."

"On what, master?"

"On whether or not I receive more food. Gems of wisdom are not to be given without reward."

Carodyne finished his ale. In this world some things, at least, had not changed. And one thing would never change where men had money and time to kill. He rose and crossed the room to a table from which came familiar sounds. A gambler, inevitable in such a place, was busy plying his trade. Dice rattled on the smooth wood and a half-dozen men released their breaths with sounds of disgust.

"Your luck is bad, gentlemen," said the gambler in a smooth voice. "But your bad luck is my good fortune." He looked up from where he sat behind heaped coins as Carodyne joined the crowd. He was a sharp-faced man wearing a wide-sleeved robe which fell from narrow shoulders. His eyes were dark, furtive, as wary as those of an animal. "There is no magic at work here, my friends. You bet and you throw. If you win I pay you. If you lose I take your wager. Could anything be more fair?"

Carodyne watched as a man threw down coins, picked up the leathern dice cup and threw the cubes. The markings were familiar, the game the same as he had played on a hundred worlds. As the man turned away, cursing his bad luck, Carodyne took his place.

The gambler looked at the metal link he threw on the table, matched it with a pile of coins, loaded the cup and passed it over. "A seven," he cried as the dice came to rest. "You win. Again?"

Carodyne nodded, watching as the man scooped up the dice and reloaded the cup. He threw and heard a sharp intake of breath from the watchers as the dice settled to show a four. A man slammed money on the table.

"I bet that he doesn't make it!"

"I'll bet that he does!"

Carodyne ignored the babble as he watched the hands of the gambler. Again he threw and made a seven.

"Bad luck, sir." The gambler raked in the bets. "Again?"

Carodyne threw down more links from the chain. He lost, doubled the bet and lost again. Once more and he was convinced the man was cheating. Slowly he dropped the last of the chain, the links rattling as they hit the table.

"A heavy wager, sir." The gambler wet his lips with the tip of his tongue. "Rarely have I seen a man so determined to win."

"You can match it?"

The lost links together with a heap of coins were pushed forward. "With ease. Throw when you will."

The dice bounced, settled, showed a nine. The gambler reached for them and froze as Carodyne leaned forward and gripped his wrist.

"Sir?"

Carodyne tightened his fingers. The trapped hand grew white, bloodless, four cubes falling as he shook the hand.

A man swore deep in his throat. "A switch! He was changing the dice!"

"Not so!" The gambler was quick to find a defense. "He palmed them on me. You all saw it. As he gripped my hand he let them fall."

With his free hand Carodyne swept up the cubes. "Fetch water," he ordered. "A bucket." He waited as a serving girl raced to obey. As she set down the container he held the four dice to the surface and let them fall. "Pick those which show a seven," he said to a scarred man. "Drop them again. Let them fall slowly and tell me what they show."

The man squinted. "A seven."

"The laws of chance," the gambler protested. "What does it prove?"

"As yet nothing," admitted Carodyne. "But if they continue to show that number I'll be tempted to think they are loaded. If so they brand you a cheat." He spoke to the scarred man. "Try them again. Three times. We must be fair."

The gambler jerked at his trapped wrist. "Fair? I'll be fair. You have lost some money, well, take it back. If a man can't lose then he shouldn't play."

He was brave with the courage of a cornered rat.

Carodyne waited, listened to the splash of water, the growls of the man at the bucket.

"Seven. Always a seven. Fifteen obols I've lost tonight and

now I know why. The louse cheated. He should be thrown into the storm to feed the wolves. Right, lads?"

Panic gave the gambler strength. He reared from his chair, his free hand darting within his robe, reappearing with a thin knife, the blade dull and stained with ugly smears. It swept towards Carodyne's cheek in a vicious slash, barely missing as he jerked backwards. Before it could cut again he had seized the knife hand, half falling over the table as he pushed the blade towards the wood. He felt it touch his left sleeve and heard a sharp intake of breath followed by a rattling sigh. Straightening he looked at the face of the gambler. It was empty, dead.

"Poisoned," said Deltmar. He had appeared out of nowhere, warned by the serving girls that trouble was brewing. "See?"

Carodyne looked at the hand which he had held, the cut on one finger.

"Gamblers," said Deltmar. "Usually I don't mind them or their ways but this one was greedy. Well, he has paid for it. Killed with his own knife, a vicious thing at best." He picked it up in a rag and carried it to the fire, throwing it into the flames, watching for a moment before returning to where Carodyne was reassembling his chain.

"You were lucky," he said. "But more than that you guessed what he was about to do. Well, I guess a mercenary has to develop some instinct for danger if he hopes to survive. At least you made a profit."

A mercenary? Carodyne swept up the heap of chains, his face impassive. So that's what he appeared to be, and the innkeeper would know his types. A soldier of fortune offering his word and skill for sale to any prepared to pay. A man of accepted violence which was why those who had played with the gambler stood watching him, envious but making no attempt to claim what they had lost.

Metal rang as he threw a shower of coins on the table. A half of what he had scooped up.

"Share this," he said. "Take what you have lost and spend what you find over. Wine for all."

Deltmar grinned. "A generous act, master. It will be appreciated. That's what I like about you mercenaries. You live hard and play rough but you can be trusted to bring profit to the inn." He lowered his voice as serving girls came to fill outthrust tankards. "And profit, also to yourself perhaps. When you dealt with the gambler you were observed. Did you know you had an audience?"

"You?"

"Bulan Ukand. He was watching from the gallery. He wants to see you." He smiled as Carodyne hesitated. "What can you lose? He is a rich merchant and could be of use to a man in your profession. If you seek employment it could be waiting. At least there will be wine of the finest vintage. I bring you his invitation to join him in a draft."

Bulan Ukand occupied a room on the uppermost level, a snug place paneled with silver-grained wood, a fire of scented logs providing warmth and glowing color. He was old, wizened, his slight body muffled in a robe of lustrous fur. More fur warmed his skull, a round cap edged with silk. His hands were the claws of a bird, each finger heavy with gems.

Around him stood bales and bundles, tight-bound and thick with unfamiliar symbols. To one side stood an inlaid table bearing a crystal lamp and a stone flagon. It contained wine as thick as oil and so deeply red as to be almost black.

"From Eeagan," he said as Carodyne studied it against the light. "They made a thousand bottles a century ago and this is one of the last. I drink to your health."

"And to yours," said Carodyne. The wine was velvet soft to his tongue, filling his mouth with the scent of roses before slipping down his throat to fill his stomach with summer warmth.

"I saw you question the gambler." Bulan set down his goblet and touched his lips with a square of fabric. "And I understand that you killed him."

"By accident."

"Or unsuspected intent. No matter, the man was a fool. Greed made him careless. He should have let you win more often than he did." He picked up his goblet and sipped at the wine. "Tell me," he said abruptly. "Do you have knowledge of the country to the north and east?"

"No."

"The land of Kedash and beyond?"

Carodyne shook his head. "Why do you ask?"

"I am going there. I have a guide I think I can trust and men to protect me. I would like to add you to their number. I take it that you are free to accept such service?"

"That depends." Carodyne looked at the bundles standing on the floor. Too precious to be trusted to Deltmar's care? "A trading expedition?"

"You could call it that. I intend to reach Kedash and beyond. To Gualek," he added softly. "The Golden. You think me a fool?"

"No," said Carodyne, and meant it. Whatever the merchant was, no man could call him that. But Gualek? "I've never heard of it," he said honestly.

"Not even by rumor?"

"No."

"You surprise me." Bulan reached for his wine. "I would have thought otherwise, but no matter. It is a city in which all things can be found. A place of great achievement in which men live like gods. I am an old man as you can see and soon I must die. Does it surprise you to learn that I fear death? That, if it were in my power, I would chose to live on for eternity? I have consulted a hundred men of great wisdom, sorcerers, necromancers, magicians of the highest order. None can help me but all agree on one thing. Only in Gualek can I find the means to extend my years. I must reach the city and buy the secret."

Carodyne said, dryly, "And if they won't sell?"

"They will. They must." Bulan was confident with a lifetime of experience. "I am a trader and know my business. All things have a price. For what I hope to find I am willing to give all I own."

A realist if nothing else, thought Carodyne. Without life wealth was useless, a thing few men realized until it was too late. And Gualek seemed an interesting place. A city in which all things could be found. Himself, perhaps? Was this a hint, a push in the direction he was supposed to go?

He said, "How long will this journey take?"

"Does it matter? We search until we find. I will pay well for the use of your sword and the shrewdness of your mind. Equal to what I pay the captain of my guard. You agree?"

Bulan smiled as Carodyne nodded. "Good. We leave at the breaking of the storm. Now let us have a final drink to seal the bargain."

7

DRAMAUT was annoyed. The captain of the merchant's bodyguard had a fine sense of procedure and for ten days now he had nursed a grievance. It had been that long since they had left the inn, forcing their way through snow, then slush, now over stoney ground, through scrub which burned with thick smoke and vile smells. His horse stumbled and he swore, lifting his voice to yell at the men riding beside the litter, the pack animals strung out behind.

"Keep alert there! Close in at the rear. Damn you, close in!"

It helped but not enough, the grievance remained. From beneath the rim of his helmet he looked ahead to where Carodyne rode with the guide. He should have been consulted before the man had been hired. His knowledge used to determine fitness and worth. There should have been wine and long discourse, his own importance recognized and his verdict taken. Instead the merchant had simply announced the fact and left him to make the best of it.

He rode, brooding, staring at the figures ahead. There was something wrong with the mercenary. He kept too much to himself, staying close to the guide who was more animal than man, talking little and saying nothing about his past. And that, in the captain's experience, was wrong. Mercenaries were, by nature, boastful men, quick to anger, ready to quarrel and considering themselves better than most. Fighters

58

who drank deep and gambled often. He was one himself and he should know.

He glanced at the sky. It was getting late, his bones ached and his stomach was empty. Ten days from the soft comfort of the inn where he had eaten well and slept soft and who knew how much longer they would travel before such comfort came his way again? And there had been a girl. Another day and she would have been his. Damn the storm which had ended too soon!

Carodyne heard the shouts as the captain yelled again at his men and turned in his saddle to look at the straggling line. Dramaut was right to enforce discipline. Here, where the ground was open, they had little to fear from raiders, but ahead was another matter. Then quick obedience could mean the difference between life and death, and the captain was too shrewd a warrior to allow slackness to develop into a habit.

He looked ahead to where the ground fell away into a thickly wooded valley rising to a distant ridge. To the guide he said, "What lies beyond?"

"The warm lands. A good place to camp."

"Can we reach it before dark?"

The guide nodded. He was a stunted creature dressed in a tatter of furs, his eyes furtive, his face flat and with flaring nostrils. Carodyne's job, as agreed with the merchant, was to ride with him. To protect him if he was attacked and to kill him if he tried to desert.

As they rode down the slope he said, casually, "Life is hard. If a man had the chance to get rich very quickly he would be a fool not to take it. Do you agree?"

A grunt was his answer.

"Of course he would need help," continued Carodyne. "One man could never do it alone. Not even two. But if a man had a good friend to watch out for him it would help."

"To have a friend is always good," said the guide. "I've been watching you. You aren't like the others. You stay alone, like me. Maybe we should stick together. Be partners."

"Yes," said Carodyne. "Or brothers."

"Do you have brothers?"

"No."

"I have. Three of them. One tried to kill me and the others stole my horse, my field and my woman. To hell with brothers. A partner is best. You can pick him. You can't a brother."

The woods closed about them, shadowed, mysterious, the trees thick with underbrush and clumps of thorn. It opened as they rode, and Carodyne paused on the ridge to rest his horse. Before him the ground fell away to a flat area misted with vapor.

"The warm lands," said the guide. "There's a place about a mile to the left where we can descend. You head for it while I go back to the column."

To report to the merchant? Carodyne doubted it. He had touched the man's greed and gained his wary trust, establishing a contact he had worked for days to make. If the man had any ideas about robbing the merchant, he wouldn't want to betray a potential ally.

That night they rested in comfort, sprawled on soft grass beneath feathery trees. Strips of meat hung on peeled wands over glowing fires. Someone had produced a flagon and the scent of mulled wine rose above that of roasting flesh. Two men had wrestled, veins knotted in their temples, free hands scrabbling the dirt. A short man sat cross-legged sharpening his sword. Another used a heated poniard to sear a pattern on his buckler. Two others threw dice in a helmet. A normal scene at any camp of such a nature.

Crossing to the fire Carodyne lifted a wand of meat, blew on the smoking scraps and bit into the smoking flesh. Curiously he looked at the soldier busy with his poniard and shield. He was burning an intricate design into the metal-studded leather, working from a drawing on a scrap of parchment. He thrust the cooling poniard back into the flames and met Carodyne's eyes.

"A rune of great power," he explained. "I bought it from a sorcerer at the inn. It will give protection against the attacks of birds, ghosts, vampires and harmful spells. And the time is fortuitous for its inscription. No moon, an absence of women, in a place untainted by the hand of man. If you wish to copy it the fee would be small."

"No thanks," said Carodyne. "I have my own defenses."

"Can a man have too many?" The soldier lifted the poniard, tested it, thrust it back into the flames. "Who knows what dangers can spring from darkness? Ghouls, demons, spirits hungry for the warmth of blood. Brigands armed with weapons of magic. On such a journey as this a man needs more than his sword."

"Who says so?" Dramaut came stalking from the shadows. He had doffed his cloak and helmet and his reddish hair rose in a mass of short spikes over his skull. Muscle bulged beneath the ringed hauberk. "Sorcery," he sneered. "Rely on that for protection and you'll fall at the first encounter. It's a thing for women and fools. Crones muttering spells and wizards who frighten children. The best magic is a sharpened blade, the best protection leather and steel."

"You can't be sure of that," protested the soldier. "I've seen a man killed by a pointing stick. A sorcerer did it at Zelmaya. And I've seen men eat fire and thrust knives into their flesh and not bleed. What else is that but magic?"

"I don't give a damn what it is but I want none of it here!" Dramaut stood, glaring. "You're fighting men and remember it. Now get some rest—we leave three hours before dawn."

Carodyne followed the captain as he moved away. "So soon?"

"You want to argue about it?"

"The men are tired and the beasts jaded. There will be no moon and starlight is deceptive. You know that."

"I know it but I'm not giving the orders. He is." Dramaut jerked his thumb to where the tent of Bulan Ukand shone with a soft luminescence. "He's crazy for speed. Anyone would think we had an army at our heels. I tried to tell him but he wouldn't listen." He added, bitterly, "Maybe you should talk to him. He takes no notice of me."

Carodyne sensed the grievance and guessed at the cause. "He should. I know he thinks a lot of you. The only reason I took service with the merchant was because you were his captain."

"He should have consulted me."

"I know it and so does he. He felt guilty about not asking your advice, but it was late and a decision had to be made. All he really wants me for is to handle the guide. And you know what these merchants are, they think one sword is as good as another. They don't realize that men who fight together have to be careful."

"I didn't know that," said the captain, mollified. "We should have spoken before."

"With you so busy and me having to watch the guide?" Carodyne shrugged. "Where was the need? You knew that you had the final decision. When you accepted me I thought you understood."

Dramaut beamed. At least the man was respectful and recognized who was really in command. And he could afford to be generous.

"You've ridden hard since we left the inn. There's no need for you to stand watch tonight. Get some sleep while you can."

It was hard to rest. After a few hours Carodyne rose and prowled the camp like a disconsolate ghost. He felt restless, filled with a vague disquiet, halting for long periods as his eyes probed the darkness. There was no wind, the feathery fronds of the trees hung like lace from their branches and only the heavy breathing of sleeping men and the occasional movement of a horse broke the silence.

He found himself nodding, jerking awake with his mind full of disjointed images, great towers of steel shining in the glare of emerald suns, roads of blinding white, empty of traffic, winding for countless miles. Crystals, turning, shining, changing shape, toppling heaps of bleached bones and things which moved and watched from the depths of shadowed caverns. He gulped air, conscious of the pounding of his heart, the strange constriction of his chest. Walking he forced his mind to become active, studying the region in which they had camped.

He could see little but remembered the view gained from the ridge. A flat land steaming with vapor, warm, almost hot when compared to the valley and the land beyond. A subsistence of the ground probably caused by subterranean volcanic activity. Underground heat would account for the warmth and the vapor. But it was odd that no one had farmed it. Odder still that the night was so quiet. There should have been a host of little sounds. Night-calls from nocturnal birds, the rustle of small animals in the grass, even the stridulation of insects.

Carodyne turned and ran towards the fire. Sparks flew as he raked the embers with his boot, the coals burning with a dull blue luminescence. He flung a handful of twigs on the fire and blew them into life. The flames rose reluctantly, dim and edged with blue. In the light he ran to where the nearest man lay sleeping.

"Up!" He slapped the flaccid cheeks. "Up, damn you! Up!"

The man groaned, working his mouth. Water stood in an urn nearby. Carodyne snatched it, flung it over the vacant features. Grimly he reached down and dug his fingers into tender flesh. The man reared, screaming like an injured horse.

"Rise! Get up! Wake the others!"

Carodyne ran to another sleeping figure, woke him, ran to the third. Snatching up two swords he dashed their blades together, the harsh clanging sounding over the camp, the most effective sound he knew to wake fighting men.

Dramaut's bull-roar echoed over the sound and the captain, red-eyed and swaying, came lurching from where he had slept.

"To arms!" he yelled, then clutched at his temples. "My head! What's happening? Are we under attack?"

"Get the men on their feet." Carodyne threw down the swords. "Keep them walking until they recover and then let's get out of here."

"Run?" Dramaut's sword whined from its sheath. "Without a fight? Where is the enemy?"

"Here. All around you. Something you can't kill."

"Ghosts? Are we the victims of sorcery?"

He glared around the camp. Men were on their feet, some helping others, all staggering as if bemused. A score of mercenaries together with a dozen servants. Beside the fire a man retched, shuddering at the spasms, his face purple. A servant fell as he headed towards the horses and continued his journey at a crawl. Carodyne ran towards him, set him on his feet and leaned him against the bole of a tree.

"Stay there," he ordered. "If you fall down get up again immediately. If you stay down you'll die."

"Master? What is happening?"

Carodyne ignored the man, returning to where the captain, sword in hand, yelled orders. "Light some more fires! Keep moving, you! Up, damn you, I'll cut the feet off the first man who falls! Move and keep moving." To Carodyne he said, "What is it? Magic?"

"Gas. There are no insects and in a place as warm and fertile as this there should be. Vapor is coming from the ground. There is no wind so it rose high. Anyone close to the dirt would quickly be overcome."

"Sorcery!" Dramaut slammed his sword back into its sheath. "I knew this place was too good to be true. A trap set by malevolent demons to snare honest men. But you? How did you escape?"

"Luck, I guess. Now get ready to break camp while I go and warn the merchant."

Bulan Ukand lay on a heap of furs, the bed set at an angle to the floor, his head raised so as to aid his breathing. A habit which had probably saved his life. The noise had woken him and he stared at Carodyne, his eyes sunken by fatigue so that they shone like sparks at the bottom of a well. He pursed his lips at the warning.

"Could the guide have known?"

"Probably. Or it could have been a genuine mistake. He couldn't know there would be no wind tonight. Do you want him dead?"

"Dead he cannot serve us," reminded the merchant. "And I need his knowledge. But watch him close. Has he said anything about robbing me?"

"No."

"But you think he will?"

"It's in his mind," said Carodyne. "I've tried to get close to him but without much success. He doesn't trust me and I don't blame him. If we could do without him it would be a lot safer."

"It's a risk we must take," said Bulan. He reached for a jar of water and wetted his thin lips. "Did the captain tell you we are in haste?"

"Yes. He thinks you are unwise."

"And you?"

Carodyne shrugged. "The men and the horses can travel, but what of yourself? There seems little point in dying on the journey to gain the secret of continued existence."

"True, but I have reason to hurry. There is a rendezvous which must be kept—but more of that later. You have done well—few would have recognized the danger. We must leave, you say?"

"At once."

Bulan threw back his coverings. He wore a closely knitted body garment of fine wool, a tunic and loose pants of brown silk, a sash of yellow in which rested a short dagger.

As he reached for his furs, he said, "Every circumstance holds an advantage. It lacks four hours to dawn, the men are eager to move and there is no talk of delay. An hour saved. As I said, Mark, you have done well."

8

DAWN found them on the edge of a rolling tundra over which they rode for days, eating in the saddle and crouching at night over fires made of dung. They hit a river scummed with ice, the banks scarred with giant wallows. A flock of birds rose and a shower of arrows caught many on the wing. Men cursed as they fell into the water to be gulped by unseen jaws. The river curved away and they crawled over a series of gnarled hills finally reaching a shallow valley which deepened as they approached flanking mountains.

"I don't like it," said Dramaut. He had ridden ahead to join Carodyne and the guide who had forged ahead. "Those mountains smell of danger. A good place for an ambush if anyone knew we were here. Has he said anything?"

"No."

"It isn't natural for a man to be as closemouthed as he is." The captain scowled at the guide who was busy eating something he had taken from his pouch. "I don't trust him since he found that damned place where we almost died. You should have let me take the flesh from his bones."

"And lost our guide?"

"I wouldn't have killed him, just given him something to remember."

Carodyne shrugged. It had been worth the gamble to try and win the guide's friendship, but he had said little and yielded no information. He knew nothing of Gualek. He had heard of Kedash but that was all. And he had said nothing about robbing the merchant.

He could be honest but Carodyne was convinced he wasn't. To any man the temptation would be great and he could have secret allies. If so he hadn't contacted them. Both Carodyne and the captain had seen to that, keeping watch while he slept with the horses.

He said, "How is the merchant?"

"Dying." The captain was blunt. "If we don't get to where we're going and soon he won't make it. The journey is killing him. All this push," he grumbled. "No decent food or rest. A man of his age should have more sense than to travel at such speed. And now he insists that we keep going. It will be dark before we get through the valley. If we get through it," he added darkly. "To me those mountains reek of trouble waiting and ready to spring."

The warrior's instinct which a man learned to trust or die young. As the captain wheeled to rejoin the rest of the column Carodyne spurred ahead to catch up with the guide. He was watching the sky, the circling shapes of birds. He looked down as Carodyne gripped his bridle.

"What's the idea?"

"From now on we ride together. You, me, all of us. Gathered nice and close for company."

"I thought you were my partner?"

"I was. I am. Got anything to tell me? No? Then let's ride."

The mountains grew higher. In their shadow the column hunched close, armed men close to the litter, the servants nervous as they huddled behind the flanking guards.

Carodyne rode tense in the saddle. Here, if anywhere, was the spot for an ambush. The rear of his helmet pressed against his neck as he looked up at the cliffs to either side. The rock was pitted, riddled with caves in which lurking men could hide. Even now they could be the target of drawn bows. He looked higher; more birds had joined those he had seen earlier. As he watched several of them began to drop, growing larger as they swooped down. From somewhere a whistle cut the air.

"Now," grunted the guide. He slammed heels into the side of his mount which sprang, rearing against the grip of the bridle. Off balance the guide fell, rolled, began to run down the valley.

After him charged Dramaut. He had his sword out, the blade a glittering arc of steel as he reached the running man. It touched where the head joined the body, passed through the neck and rose dripping with blood. The severed head fell to one side, the trunk continuing to run for several steps before falling over, gushing blood.

"Beware!" roared the captain as he turned to rejoin the column. "On guard!"

The sky grew dark with wings.

They came from above, from either side, great birds each larger than a horse with long necks viciously beaked. Clawed feet scrabbled at the ground as they landed with a thunder of threshing wings. Riding on each bird, mounted in saddles fastened at the base of the neck, pygmies looked like evil dolls. They carried short swords and crossbows and, suddenly, the air was thick with flying death.

Carodyne whipped out his sword as he heard the captain's shout of alarm, spurring his mount to where the big man slashed furiously at a winged opponent. He felt the stallion convulse, rearing, screaming at the bite of steel, then he was falling as the animal tore past, an arrow in its throat, another in its eye.

Rising to his feet he stared at a beaked head, the snarling face of a pygmy, the glinting tip of an aimed quarrel.

Metal clashed protectively before his face as he swept down the visor of his helmet. The quarrel struck, its point slamming into one of the eye-slots. Carodyne tore it free, leaping to one side, his sword whining down in a slash which severed the beaked head, rising to circle in a backhanded cut at the rider. Steel met flesh, dragged, broke free as the child-like body toppled from its mount.

Turning he cut again, muscles bunching in arm and shoulder. Feathers exploded from the threshing wings of a dying bird. He ran to where Dramaut fought to control his horse, arriving just as the mount threw its rider. A bird thrust its beak at the helpless man. Carodyne sliced through the neck and watched as the bird, blood hosing, took to the air in dying reflex action, its rider wailing as he fell.

A quarrel rang against his helmet, another tore at his cloak, a wing like a flail slammed against his back with bruising impact. Carodyne snatched out his dagger and sliced at the point where the wing joined the body. Leaning forward he stabbed at the rider. The point tore at the snarling face, slipped on the cheekbone and gouged into an eye.

"Back!" Yelled Dramaut. "Back!"

His sword was a wheel of light as he slashed at everything within range. An arrow tore his cheek and stained his beard with a sudden gush of blood. A pygmy screamed as his arm fell away from his body, screamed again as the sword found his heart.

Carodyne slipped as his foot trod in a pool of blood. He rolled, chopping at scaled legs, driving his dagger into scaled bellies. He heard Dramaut's roar, a shrill screaming, a sudden thunder of wings. Abruptly the immediate area was clear. He rose and met the captain's eyes.

"By God what manner of fiends are they?" Dramaut shook blood from his sword. "Demons mounted on giant birds. Never did I see the like."

Carodyne looked around. The ground was thick with feathers, blood, dead and dying birds, their riders lying like broken dolls. The air held a thick musty odor which stung the eyes.

"Quick!" roared Dramaut. "Back to back!"

Their shoulders met as fresh attackers dropped from the sky. The world turned into a red haze of blood and screaming noise. A beak smashed against Carodyne's shoulder, reared back for a second blow, fell as his sword cut through feather, skin, flesh and bone. A clawed foot kicked forward, the talons ripping at his brigandine, the blow carrying the force of a kicking horse. He doubled fighting for breath, turning to avoid a second attack, his sword slicing at yellow scales. Two curved toes fell to the ground. He heard Dramaut's yell of pain as a quarrel found his eye. It was spent, the point barely managing to penetrate the ball, but it did its work.

Blinded, mad with pain, the captain screamed in mad fury. "Death!" he yelled. "Death to all winged fiends of hell!"

Carodyne felt the sudden lightness at his back as the captain raced down the valley, sword a wheeling arc of destruction, lopped heads, guts and distorted bundles falling before his attack. The captain's insane rage had given him a respite. Gulping air into his tortured lungs Carodyne ran to where the rest of the guards stood clustered around the merchant's litter.

Too many had died. They lay sprawled in a welter of blood among the bodies of slaughtered horses, among them the limp forms of the defenseless servants shot down at the first attack. Those that were left snarled at the sky, sword and buckler in hand, arrows spent and bows useless.

Carodyne sheathed his dagger and snatched up a discarded shield, fastening it to his arm as he thrust his head into the litter. Bulan stared at him with glassy eyes, blood staining the furied collar of his robe, the shaft of a quarrel protruding from his wizened throat. The merchant was dead. His search for eternal life ended before it had really begun.

Carodyne turned, throwing up the shield and feeling the impact as a quarrel thudded into the leather and into the wood beneath. Beside him a man shrieked as a clawed foot ripped out his intestines. Another coughed and lifted a hand to his throat. A second quarrel joined the first. Vomiting blood the man fell to his knees.

Again the world became a red blur of ceaseless effort. Of targets to be cut or stabbed, menace to be sliced away, destroyed, smashed to the ground. The air stank of foul odors, of sweat and musk and newly shed blood. The world shrank to what he could see through the eye-slits of his helmet, the face of the enemy, the sense of victory as his sword cut home.

Carodyne heard the sounds of wings directly above. He leaned back squinting through his visor. A bird was hovering over his head, talons flexed ready to grab. Throwing aside the shield he sprang upwards, left hand gripping a scaled leg, the sword in his right lifting to prick at the belly.

Squawking the bird threshed the air, struggling upwards to escape the pain. Carodyne pricked it deeper, looking down as they rose. Below the fight was almost over. Even as he watched the last of the soldiers fell.

The ground began to rise and he stabbed upwards again, viciously, turning the point of his blade. Wings thundered with failing energy as the bird carried him down the valley away from the shambles. Above the rider twittered with helpless rage, unable to bring his crossbow to bear, his sword too short to reach the unwanted passenger.

Carodyne landed running, rock slapping hard against the soles of his boots. He turned as the dying bird hit the ground, cutting twice, the heads of bird and rider falling in a shower of blood. Breathing deep he raised the visor and looked back up the valley. The trail curved, the shambles out of sight, the air clear of enemies. Now was as good a time as any to make his escape.

He found Dramaut just as it was growing dark. The man leaned against a boulder, muttering in pain. Blood stained his cheek and beard, rested in brown flakes on the collar of his cloak, the neck of his hauberk. He had removed the quarrel but the injured eye was ruined.

He drew in his breath with a hiss of pain as Carodyne examined the wound. "God, but it hurts! A sword through the guts would have pained me less."

"You don't know that," said Carodyne dryly. "One thing for sure, such a wound would have killed you, this will not." He slapped the captain on the shoulder. "It isn't so bad. One eye will serve as well as two until you can get a replacement."

"A replacement? A new eye?" Dramaut stared his disbelief. "What sorcerer could accomplish that? Where could I find such a man?"

Old habits of thought had betrayed him. He should have known that replacement surgery was unknown on this world. Carodyne said, "In Gualek, perhaps. If the merchant was to be believed all things can be found there. Why not a new eye?"

"The merchant." Dramaut scowled at his bloodstained gauntlets. "I failed him. I was crazed with pain and I ran amok. But I ran in the wrong direction. My place was with my men beside the litter."

"Thank the gods who guided your feet," said Carodyne. "They saved your life."

"And my honor?"

"What use is honor to the dead? You're alive and should be thankful. Now let's get moving."

Mist rose as they continued down the valley. It grew thicker as the night deepened, coiling, swirling as if with a life of its own, taking odd and grotesque shapes. Dramaut hesitated, finally coming to a halt.

"I don't like this," he protested. "The air holds the stink of sorcery. Let us wait until day."

Carodyne was impatient. "We have no food and no water. If we build a fire we'll attract those raiders and we're in no state for another battle. And what's all this talk of sorcery? I thought you didn't believe in it."

"That was for the benefit of the men," said the captain. "But all men know that sorcery is real and magicians powerful. A demon could be lurking ahead ready to pounce."

"If it is we'll cut it down," said Carodyne. "But there's nothing to be afraid of. The merchant intended to travel through this valley and he was no fool. And if anything lay ahead the guide would have known about it."

"Maybe he did." Dramaut spat at the thought of the man. "I should have questioned him while I had the chance. A twisted cord and a slow fire would have loosened his tongue. If you hadn't stopped me the merchant would be alive now."

"I doubt it. Those raiders would have seen us in any case." Carodyne stepped ahead. "Come on now and follow close."

It grew darker, the mist thickening so that the captain had to tread almost on Carodyne's heels to keep him in view. A sound came from the right, a thin chittering, and a scurry of small creatures ran across the path, swarming over their boots and vanishing as quickly as they had appeared.

Dramaut's sword shined from its scabbard. "Demons," he muttered.

"Mice."

71

"Maybe so—but running from what?"

Carodyne drew the dagger from its sheath. The captain was a prey to imagined fears, yet it was his world and the fears need not be without foundation. Mice could run from a larger predator.

The darkness increased until they were walking blind, the mist thickening to a clammy fog which deadened sound so that their boots trod as if on cotton wool. Carodyne felt something tug at his cloak and jumped to one side, feeling thorns rip at the material. A bush. There would be others. They must have left the rocky valley and be heading into an open plain.

He bumped into something soft and round. Behind him he heard Dramaut's bull-roar, the swish of his sword. He sprang to one side as the blade slashed down. And the universe exploded in a gush of light.

9

YELLOW light spilled from the glowing heart of a faceted crystal suspended in chains of gold. It filled the interior of the tent with a soft light which gilded the rough fabric of the walls, the supports, the couch on which he lay. Carodyne sat upright. His head swam and he felt a sudden nausea. An urn of water stood on the beaten dirt of the floor, and he lifted it in both hands, drinking, letting the cold liquid gush over his head. Cautiously he probed the thick mass of his hair, finding nothing. Whatever had caused the sudden flash of light and the following unconsciousness hadn't been a blow on the head.

He looked around. The tent held little, a low table, the couch, a chest, open and containing various jars and pots of glass and earthenware. He saw no sign of his helmet, cloak, brigandine or weapon belt. Rising he looked under the couch finding nothing but the dirt floor. When he straightened he was not alone.

A man stood against the wall of the tent. He was tall, thin, his face deeply lined. His green eyes were slanted and held a peculiar intensity. His ears were small and tight against his shaven skull. Jewels shone on his fingers and his cowled robe was of ebon silk embroidered with esoteric symbols in luminous silver.

Quietly he said, "I am Albasar, socerer to King Feya, bound to Marash for my power." He gestured towards the sigil tattooed on his forehead. "And you?"

"Carodyne. Mark Carodyne."

"A mercenary?"

"I guess you could call me that. What happened?"

"You guess?" Albasar frowned. "Don't you know?"

"I'm a mercenary," said Carodyne. "I was working for the merchant Bulan Ukand. We were attacked and I managed to escape with a companion. Where is he?"

"Dead."

So Dramaut had follwed his men. Carodyne felt a vague regret; he had liked the big man with his roaring voice and simple ways. "What killed him?"

"The power of elemental demons. By great sorcery they were trapped and held in containers of skin, suspended on bushes for safety and guarded by armed men. You must have stumbled on them in the fog."

Carodyne remembered the yell, the swish of the captain's sword as he lashed in panic at something soft and round. Explosives, perhaps? The concussion of the blast must have knocked him unconscious.

He said, dryly, "That's dangerous stuff to have around."

"Which is why it was placed well from the camp. The guards found you and brought you both to my tent. My skill saved you but could do nothing for the other." Albasar paused and added, "You do not seem shaken by your near escape. Most men would be terrified lest the demons they had released had marked their soul."

"I've handled explosives before."

73

"Explosives?" The sorcerer looked puzzled. "The word is strange to me."

"The power of elemental demons," said Carodyne. "The next time you get some keep it cool. Place the skins in tubs of iced water. Was it an oily liquid very sensitive to impact?"

"How did you know that? Are you a magician?"

Nitroglycerine, thought Carodyne. A discovery made, perhaps, by some alchemist, its power naturally attributed to demons by people who believed in sorcery. Instinct warned him to be careful. Too much knowledge could be dangerous when displayed to those who would think he was possessed of some magic power.

Carefully he said, "I saw something like it a long time ago. Then a way was found to make it safe, to lock the demons in a stronger prison. Take some fuller's earth, the white powder used for cleaning garments, and let it soak up the liquid."

Dynamite would need detonators but it was a lot safer to have lying around.

"I shall remember that," said Albasar. "But now we have no need of the precaution. The demons are all fled. Now come, the king awaits your presence."

He was a man as tall as the sorcerer but broad and younger by half. He wore a complete suit of silvered mail covered with a surcoat of blazing crimson bearing the snarling mask of a tiger in yellow. His head was bare, square-cut hair framing a hard, aquiline face, and he moved with the lithe restlessness of a cat.

"You!" he snapped as Carodyne entered with the sorcerer. "Talk! Tell me what happened." He listened as Carodyne told of the journey from the inn, scowling, pacing the tent which was five times larger than the other. "So the merchant is dead and all his goods lost. Damn him for a fool! He should never have trusted the guide. Such men know how to signal with odorous foods. If it hadn't been for you he would have escaped later to share in the loot. Well, what is done cannot be undone." He struck a gong. "Wine," he ordered as a soldier answered the summons. "And double the guard."

The wine came in a brass amphora together with goblets of pewter.

"We have no money," Feya explained as he poured. He

handed Carodyne one of the goblets, Albasar refused another. "The merchant had money and used it to aid my enterprise. He was to have joined us with more. If the men learn he is dead there will be trouble. Unless you keep silent I will have you impaled at dawn."

"I won't talk." Carodyne tasted the wine; it was thin, almost sour. "He spoke of Gualek, the Golden City. He wanted to find it."

"That was our bargain. He was to help me and I to help him. He told you the details?"

"No, only of the city and what he hoped to find there. Does it really exist?"

"It could. If it does it must lie beyond Kedash—or so Bulan Ukand believed." Feya poured himself more wine. "Know this—I am the true king of Kedash. The lawful king of both city and plain. I have a sister, may God rot her soul, a woman cursed with pride and ambition. By black sorcery she conspired against me to steal my throne. The priests of Kanin aided her for reasons of their own. Enough to say that in one night of terror my guards were killed and I imprisoned. Loyal slaves opened the way to my escape. Now I return."

"To recapture your city?"

"That and to wreak vengeance on Iztima and those who aided her."

Carodyne made a pretense of studying his wine. The situation, he guessed, was normal enough on a world where primitive customs ruled and magic was accepted as a reality, even if the magic appeared to be a matter of terminology rather than anything else. But what had the problems of the king to do with his own?

Albasar said, quietly, "You could help us, Mark."

"How?"

"You are a man of unusual power. My sorcery tells me that. While you lay in my tent I examined the line of your life. It contains a mystery which I am unable to resolve. Yet one thing I know. In you lies great power and, perhaps, great sorcery."

Another push in the direction he should take? Carodyne drank some of the thin wine. He could go with the king or make his own way—but to where? To a man lost in a forest

75

any signpost was better than none. He felt his anger rise at the thought of being manipulated, to be used as a toy by the players of the Omphalos, but he was trapped in this world and could only escape if he found himself—whatever that might mean.

"I need men," said Feya abruptly. "I will be honest with you, my forces are not as good as I would like. You have the look of a fighter and you have something more than just a sword. Luck, skill, shrewdness, the things the merchant needed. I need them too. Will you accept my service?"

"For how long?"

"Until Kedash is mine or I am dead. As time is measured that will not be long. Right, sorcerer?"

Albasar nodded. "We dare delay no longer, my lord. Time is running out. Each hour adds to the odds against you and favors the black arts of she who sits on your throne."

The king emptied his goblet. "I'll make you the captain of a hundred," he said to Carodyne. "When Kedash is mine there will be gold and jewels and fair maids for your pleas* A mansion and land to call your own. A command in service if you wish and your own road to travel if you prefer. Come, man, where else could you hope for such high reward?"

A gambler's stake, thought Carodyne. Win all or get nothing, but what had he to lose?

"You are generous, my lord. Until Kedash has fallen?"

"Or until I am dead. If you agree give me your hand."

Carodyne felt the fingers close over his own as Albasar repeated the terms and gave the oath. Feya laughed as the hands fell apart.

"Good," he said. "I have the feeling that you will do me a great service. Now that you are one of us tell me what you think of my plan."

A map lay on a table. Feya tapped it with a finger. "We are here. This is the Elkite Sea. We could make our way by land but the journey would be long and the dangers many. So we will travel by sea to a place close to Kedash. Surprise and speed are our best hope of success, essential now that we have lost what the merchant carried. You agree?"

"No army can have better weapons than those," admitted

76

Carodyne. "But alone they aren't enough. What of the ships, the men to work them, food and supplies for the campaign?"

"The ships are here waiting to be used. The sailors also, and we shall have support from within the city once we arrive." The king yawned, revealing strong white teeth. "To bed," he ordered. "Rest while you've got the chance. We leave with the tide."

Carodyne had no desire for sleep. Instead he wandered from the tent and examined the camp. It was smaller than he'd expected, lines of men close-huddled on the ground, a few watch fires illuminating armed guards, a few wandering patrols.

A silver-flecked shadow loomed at his side.

"You are restless," said Albasar. "Troubled. I can sense it in your mind."

"Then you can guess the cause." Carodyne gestured at the camp. "Does the king hope to win a throne with so few?"

"He told you that there will be help from within the city."

"You believe that?"

"It is not my place to call the king a liar."

Nor mine, thought Carodyne. Not when he is surrounded by armed men and talks of impalement at dawn. "He could be misinformed. In my experience those who rely on others seldom succeed. Yours too, I think. Just what is this Kedash like?"

"If you would learn follow me."

A guard straightened as they approached the sorcerer's tent. It was half the size of the king's, the fabric decorated with a variety of symbols, many of them the same as Bulan Ukand had used on his bundles. They hadn't helped the merchant, and Carodyne wondered if they could help anyone else. Inside a glowing jewel similar to the one he had seen on waking filled the enclosure with a soft radiance. A brazier emitted a red glow, smoke rising as Albasar threw a pinch of powder into the coals. It twisted, coiling as the sorcerer stepped to where a bowl of water stood on a brazen tripod.

It was about a foot wide, the surface tranquil, seeming to be coated with oil so that it reflected a rainbow of light. Albasar stood before it, hands extended so they shadowed the bowl, head tilted and lips moving in a silent incantation.

The water rippled from unseen forces.

Carodyne stared down at a city.

It looked minute, a thing built for the pleasure of children and seen from the eyes of a bird. It rested on the edge of a plain and was flanked by soaring peaks tipped with snow, mountains which ran to either side apparently impossible to climb. Curtain walls of crenellated stone ran between towers topped with conical roofs. Inside the walls ran a maze of alleys, streets, narrow roads. Rearing from one side of an open plaza a fortresslike palace dominated the scene. From its flat roof rose a coiling spiral of smoke.

"Kedash," said Albasar quietly. "It guards the pass into the lands beyond."

"Where Gualek is supposed to lie?"

"That is so. The mountains run to either side enclosing a vast land. The city itself, as you see, lies in a pocket of the mountains. There is a pass, not easy, but the only one to the place beyond."

Carodyne could realize its importance. But why hadn't the merchant contacted the city direct, using his wealth to buy free passage from the present occupier of the throne.

"The queen trusts no one," said Albasar when he asked. "No strangers are allowed within the land on pain of death. Traders are discouraged by impalement. Wandering monks are crucified. Mercenaries are flayed alive." He pointed to the fortress. "This was old Kedash. Now the building is both the palace and the temple. Once Marash was worshiped there. Now the devotees of Kanin sully the sacred stones with their degraded rites."

"It won't be easy to take," said Carodyne. "Those walls are high and strong."

"Marash will aid us."

"I'd rather have siege engines and men to work them." Carodyne studied the image. There was no moat but a deep trench had been gouged from the hard ground before the city. It would, he guessed, hold venomous reptiles and a profusion of poisonous insects. "How about water? Are there any wells?"

"Yes."

And there would be food stored in underground chambers against a time of siege. "How about the queen?"

78

Again the sorcerer extended his hands. The image dissolved, took new shape, a room as seen from a few feet above the floor. A bed occupied one wall, furs lay scattered on a floor of polished onyx, light streamed from gems set in mounts of gold and silver. From within the bowl a woman faced them brushing her hair.

Velvet skin caught the light and threw it back with rose-petal softness from the rounded shoulders and swelling breasts. She wore a robe of shimmering silver, low on the front and tight to waist and thighs. Her lips were red and full with sensuosity. Long, dark lashes sheltered her eyes. The lustrous tresses of her golden hair streamed down to her waist.

"Iztima, present queen of Kedash, sister to my lord the king." The voice of Albasar was low. "A dangerous woman despite her beauty. The High Priest of Kanin is her constant advisor, lending her the strength of his sorcery in return for the freedom to practice his diabolic arts."

The woman in the image smiled, throwing back her head to expose the lines of her throat. She leaned forward and touched the corner of an eye and Carodyne realized that she sat before a mirror and they saw her as if they stood behind it.

Magic? No device he knew could reach out and capture an image from a closed room. He looked at the sorcerer with new respect. Did the man have the power to bend space by means of his incantations and esoteric trappery? Or was he merely using the bowl of water to reflect the images of his own mind? And, if he had such mental power, who knew its limitations?

He said, "The king was quick to offer me a command. Had you influenced him?"

"I sowed the seed while you were asleep."

"And those bags you hung on the bushes. Did you make what they contained?"

"Marash does not deal with instruments of wanton destruction. Her servants do not trade with malignant demons. They were purchased from the wizards of Lotagh." Albasar seemed amused. He said, "You have seen something beyond your understanding. Or perhaps it would be better to say something you do not understand. There are many mysteries in the world. No man can know them all."

Carodyne looked at the bowl. The water showed only the shimmer of oil. "If you can see at a distance you could have followed the merchant on his journey. You could have warned him, perhaps, sent men to help against the raiders. If you had he could be alive now."

"No man can escape his destiny. If he is meant to die his life will terminate no matter how many guards ring his couch."

"You talk as if no man is free."

"No man is," said Albasar firmly. "Small things he can do at will; warm his hands at a fire or remain in the cold, drink wine or water, touch his hair or stroke his face, walk or run, dress how he pleases and eat what he chooses. But other things are controlled by the arbiters of his fate. He has no choice as to where he is born, none as to when he will die. And he moves at the direction of powers impossible to comprehend. Think a moment. Why was the king thrown from his city? What caused his sister to usurp the throne. What caused the storm which delayed the merchant at the inn so that you could join his service? Could it not be that all these things happened to bring you here at this time and place ready and able to take service with the king?"

The man was a philosopher; perhaps philosophy and sorcery were much the same in this world. Certainly he was a thinker and could be used. Carodyne said, "Would you answer a question for me?"

"What is it?"

"How can a man find himself?"

The green eyes widened a little, then veiled as the sorcerer stood deep in thought. Finally he said, "The question you ask has plagued men of wisdom for countless years. How does a man find himself? He looks down and he is there. But is he the thing he looks at or is he seeing through other eyes? If so how would he know? And what of his nature, his inner being? Has a man found himself if he is not happy at his appointed task? Can a man who tends flocks be sure he should not have sailed ships? The question holds unsuspected complexities when approached with a discerning mind. For example, my hand is me, but if I cut it off I do not die, so how can it be me? And if it is a part of myself, and I lost it, do I find myself when finding it again?"

"I didn't want a metaphysical discussion," said Carodyne impatiently. "Assume a man knows who and what he is. Yet he still has to find himself. What then?"

"A riddle?"

"Call it that if you like. Can you read it?"

"For such a man to find himself he must look at the truth." Albasar threw another pinch of powder into the brazier. "And, as each man carries his own truth, how would he do that?"

"Look at himself," said Carodyne. "In a mirror?"

"A mirror does not reveal the truth. The image is a distorted picture of a man. What he does with his right hand the image does with its left. Truth is not to be found in an ordinary mirror. But if there was one which made no such distortion? If it gave a perfect likeness?" Albasar spread his hands. "There is the answer to your riddle. For a man to find himself he must look into the mirror of truth."

10

RAIN came with the morning light, a steady downpour which extinguished the fires and clung in glistening droplets to the accouterments of the men as they broke camp ready to embark. They were a motley crew. Leather and cloaks of wool, hauberks of interlinked rings, shirts of mail, quilted padding with here and there a sheen of burnished plate. The weapons were as varied as the armor—cross-hilted swords, scimitars, tulwars, long-handled axes and viciously spiked maces, falchions and rapiers of flexible steel. Faces, bearded and shaven, mottled and scarred, scowled from beneath the rims of a dozen types of helmet.

Carodyne found his command and piled them into one of the waiting ships; broad-beamed craft with rounded bottoms and unwieldy sails. The hulls lacked paint and stank of bilge water. The sailors were blacks with kinked hair and yellow eyes, muffled in gaudy fabrics with curved knives naked in their belts. The rain had plastered their clothing tight against their bodies, muscles standing clear as they hauled on ropes, singing a wailing chant and keeping time to the beat of a drum. Slowly the flotilla headed into the Elkite Sea.

In the tiny poop of the vessel Carodyne joined his two lieutenants. Hostig, big, blond, a giant from the north, ordered wine. He took a mouthful and spat it out with a curse.

"Damn that steward! It's watered and sour. I've a mind to slit his belly for daring to cheat fighting men."

"All men cheat if they can." Seyhat was dark, olive-skinned, clean and neatly dressed in expensive silks and armor. "It is the way of life. We rob others and are robbed in return. Each living thing lives on the efforts of another. Like fleas on a dog. The whole world is a parasite."

Hostig growled deep in his throat. "Are you calling me a flea?"

Seyhat narrowed his eyes. "And if I am?"

A thick arm banded in wide bracelets of silver dropped a big hand to the hilt of a dagger. "This flea can bite, Seyhat! Come on deck and I'll show you how."

Carodyne watched them, wondering if they were acting a part, testing him, perhaps, to study his reaction. Men like these would respect no one not stronger than themselves.

Slamming down his goblet he said, "Shut up, the pair of you! If you want to fight I'll take care of you both. Now to business. Hostig! Number your men!"

For a moment the tension held, then the big northerner shrugged. "A dozen bows, the same of axes, most have shields and all have daggers."

"Armor?"

"A few with breasts of plate, most with links of mail and a few with stiffened hide."

"Seyhat?"

"About the same. I'm a dozen short of my fifty; we had fights and desertions. A few slingers from the Iles of Katodin and some crossbowmen from Legona." The lieutenant helped himself to more wine. "In a pinch they will fight well enough but we are short of supplies."

"No food or wine," grumbled Hostig. "The king promised us plenty of both but gave us nothing." He stared at Carodyne. "I'll put it straight. I don't like to follow an unknown man. You look as you should but can you act as you must?"

"I can," said Carodyne bluntly. "Must I kill you to prove it?"

"You think you could do that?"

A dagger in the eye, thought Carodyne. A quick move over before the big man could see it coming. Or, perhaps, a finger would do as well. A stab and then a blow to the throat which would rupture the larynx. Better because it would be faster.

"Wait!" said Seyhat sharply. He had been watching Carodyne's face. "Hostig, why must you be such a fool? What kind of a mercenary are you that you can't recognize a brother? Mark is one of us and I, for one, am willing to follow him. Now relax and enjoy the wine."

Hostig grunted, toying with his goblet.

"Personally I think the gods must have fuddled my senses when I agreed to join with the king," continued Seyhat. "His promises reached the sky but words are cheap. We have less than five hundred men with which to win a throne."

"I heard talk," said Hostig. "Others were to have joined us. None came."

"One came," corrected Seyhat. "Tent walls are thin and guards curious. Our commander is a special man, loved by the gods and trusted by the king. Such a man would not see his comrades die in vain. Not when a word in the right ear could turn blood into gold." He lifted his goblet. "I drink to you, Mark Carodyne. And to success in our enterprise."

"Success," rumbled Hostig, echoing the toast.

Carodyne drank, recognizing the unspoken hint beneath the flattery. Mercenaries were casual as to their loyalties. A shrewd commander could often turn defeat into victory by changing sides at the right time. One less shrewd could easily be killed by his own men.

Putting down his goblet he rose. "Finish the wine. I'm going on deck for a breath of air."

Outside the wind had risen, sleeting the rain with cold misery on the men huddled in the waist of the ship, adding to the discomfort caused by the wallowing of the ungainly vessel. Carodyne picked his way to the quarterdeck where the captain met him with a hostile stare.

"This part of the ship is forbidden to you and yours, master. I must ask you to leave at once."

Carodyne looked around, not answering, interested in what he saw. Three men stood by the great shaft of the tiller, another squatted on his haunches staring into a bowl of water in which floated a scrap of wood bearing a sliver of metal. A crude compass, useful, perhaps, in fog, but inaccurate, especially when the ship was carrying men heavy with iron. An awning gave little protection, flapping with each gust of wind.

The captain was impatient. "Master, must I summon men to have you removed?"

He was a tough veteran of the sea, squat and padded with muscle. An old injury had torn one side of his face so that he squinted from an eye perpetually hooded. Before he could signal, Carodyne said, "My men are cold. They need hot food and wine."

"Maybe so, master, but my agreement with your king said nothing about feeding my passengers."

"Yet surely something could be arranged?" Carodyne lifted his hands and removed the chain from around his neck. Slowly he let the links fall from one hand into the palm of the other. "Hungry men make uneasy cargo. A bowl of stew would settle uneasy stomachs and make the journey more pleasant for us all?"

"My lord!" The captain bowed, all smiles. Beyond him his men took their hands from their curved daggers. "I have meat and spices from the south, food hot enough to warm the bones of the dead. It shall be arranged."

"And wine?"

"That also." The captain reached out and closed his hand over the chain. "You are a generous man, my lord. All shall be as you command. And," he added shrewdly, "I shall make certain they know the source of their good fortune."

The rain ceased, yielding to a watery sun and then, as the day passed, returned with savage winds which whipped the sea to froth and caused the vessel to rear and wallow like a stricken beast. The light grew dull, the sky taking on a coppery tinge, and the captain looked anxiously at his sails. He set a lantern on the masthead as a signal to the other vessels of the little fleet, but the answering gleams were widely scattered. As darkness fell the wind increased, sending mounds of water crashing over the gunwales. In the waist sodden men cursed with a dull fury as they bailed with their helmets.

At dawn the storm eased, the wind dying as abruptly as it had risen so that they drifted in an uneasy calm. As the light grew they entered a bank of fog, the muffling clouds of vapor closing the ship in a tiny world. Little sounds became magnified, the noise of the sailors as they padded over the deck, the creak of timbers, the splash as damaged spars were thrown overboard. In the waist the mercenaries grumbled as they dozed, restless in their wet clothing. The sails hung limp and lifeless from the yards.

The captain, haggard from fatigue, spread his hands at Carodyne's questions.

"What can I do, my lord? There is no wind. We have no sweeps. All we can do is to wait and drift with the current."

"Haven't you got any small boats we could man to tow the ship out of this fog?"

"None. They were all smashed in the storm."

"Food then? There must be something left from the chain."

The captain shrugged. "What we have I am willing to share, but it is little and mostly spoiled."

"Have it prepared," said Carodyne. "Give each man a—" He broke off, frowning, eyes narrowed as he stared into the fog. "What was that?"

"I heard nothing, my lord."

"Listen!"

It came again, a soft creaking from starboard, a scrape and the swish of something on water. Above it, like the muted beating of a heart, came a repetitious thudding.

The captain sucked in his breath. "A galley," he whispered. "The only ones using such craft are the pirates who haunt the shores of the Haddeciak Iles. The storm must have blown them far to the west—or us far to the east. May the gods grant the fog holds!"

In the waist a man dropped his helmet and swore, the sound of his curse rising above the clatter of steel.

"Silence!" The captain snarled commands at his men. "Keep them silent! Crack skulls if you must but stop all sounds!" He glanced aloft as the sailors padded away. The sails still hung without life, but now the fog seemed to be thinning, swirling as if at the touch of invisible hands. "An hour," prayed the captain. "Less as long as they don't see or hear us. Ten minutes, even; if the fog holds that long we have a chance."

Tensely they waited as the fog thinned, rising faster now, streaming in plumes as the sail gave a single flap. Before it could fill the area was suddenly clear.

"There!" The captain lifted a thick arm, pointing. "May the gods blind their sight!"

The galley was a quarter of a mile away heading to the north. It was long and low, rising high at bow and stern. A single mast bore a square-cut sail marked with the design of a snake. A yell rose from the vessel and the brazen clash of cymbal echoed over the water. Oars lashed the waves, turning the galley to present its ram to the helpless ship.

"Hostig! Seyhat!" Carodyne turned, shouting for his officers. "Send the archers aloft, the crossbowmen and slingers to the forecastle and poop. Keep the others below the gunwales until they strike. Move!"

To the captain he said, "Have you weapons of defense? Quick, man! We have little time!"

There was a catapult, crude and practically useless, the arm swung by counterweights. Carodyne watched as sailors hauled it back and loaded the cup with a stone.

"Find rag," he snapped. "Soak it in oil. Set it alight and hurl it at the galley."

The stone missed. The flaming mass of rag quenched itself in the ocean. There was no time for more. Already the galley had increased speed, the drum pounding to keep the rowers in time. Foam churned from the vicious beak of the ram, and on the forecastle men screamed with the anticipation of an easy conquest.

Carodyne ducked as an arrow whistled past his head, sent the visor of his helmet dropping before his face as another tore at his cloak.

"Now!" he yelled to his own bowmen. "Shoot!"

Arrows flickered in answer towards the galley, most falling short because of wet strings. A man standing on the advancing prow toppled backwards as a slinger sent a stone smashing into his face. Answering missiles thickened the air. An archer fell from the mast. Two crossbowmen fell where they stood. A sailor screamed as a quarrel splintered his knee.

Carodyne snarled behind his visor. The defenders were uncoordinated, verging on the edge of panic as they tried to do too many things at once. Hostig roared like a bull as he moved among them shouting commands. Seyhat, more subtle, directed his men with quiet confidence, his example spreading a degree of calmness.

The cymbals clashed again as the galley drew close, the drum reaching a crescendo, men yelling like fiends as they brandished swords and axes.

"Hold tight!" yelled Carodyne.

The ram struck.

It hit with a grinding roar, ripping into the planks and sending the ungainly sailing vessel listing far to one side. Shaken free by the impact men fell from the masts, screaming as they hit the deck or water. From the waist came a gush of water as the sea poured through the riven side. On the prow of the galley men clustered ready to spring.

Carodyne drew sword and dagger. "Hostig!" he yelled. "Seyhat! All you men in the waist! Follow me!"

He sprang to the bulwark which rose above the deck of the galley, the space between the side and the prow a hell of churning water. Without hesitation Carodyne sprang over it, boots thudding as he landed on the attacker's deck, sword a flashing arc of steel.

A man fell backwards, beard and throat slit by the razor edge. Another parried a cut and died as the dagger found his

87

unprotected armpit. A third looked blankly at the stump of his severed arm then fell to one side as Carodyne pressed forward, sword and dagger busy, the muscles of back and shoulders bunching as he smashed down opposing weapons.

He felt the thud of feet behind him and heard the roar as Hostig split a helmet and the skull beneath his heavy blade shearing through metal and bone alike. A spear flashed over his shoulder and buried its point in the chest of a man lifting a mace. Others followed as Seyhat directed their aim. A sudden volley of missiles and Carodyne found himself a third of the way along the deck of the galley. After him, yelling with blood lust, the mercenaries poured from the stricken vessel.

Like mad dogs the pirates fought back.

They had been taken by surprise thinking the ship a wallowing merchantman, easy loot and easier prey, not even worried by the archers and slingers so confident had they been of their overwhelming power. Carodyne had startled them with his surprise attack, gaining ground before they could adjust to the new situation, but now, faced with death, they fought like the wolves they were.

Cymbals clashed and the beat of the drum rose above the screams of dying men, the clash of steel. Oars foamed the water was they drew the galley away from the riven vessel, cutting off any hope of reinforcements for the men on deck. From the stern came a new wave of attackers, fresh, determined to kill or die trying, knowing they had no other choice.

Carodyne ducked as a point thrust at his visor, slashed at a leg to hamstring his opponent, rose to send his dagger into a straining throat. An axe rang from his helmet. A sword lashed at his cloak. He parried a vicious cut, slashed back in turn, rammed the pommel into a snarling face, felt the blade of his dagger hit bone. He moved constantly, almost dancing on the balls of his feet, weaving, cutting, using point and edge as the occasion arose. Around him the world was filled with screams and shouts and the gushing crimson of freshly shed blood.

And, suddenly, there was nothing before him. Only the sea, the endless waves, the empty sky.

"Over the side with them!" roared Hostig. "Clear the deck of this carrion!"

Carodyne turned, lifting the visor so as to cool his face. Around him men were busy dumping the dead over the side, the wounded, too, if they were pirates. Beyond the prow he could see the ship, listing heavily, men thick on the high bulwark. Around it fins cut the water as sharks raced to feed on the unexpected harvest.

He looked down. From head to foot he was covered in blood, the sword and dagger notched and stained in his gauntleted hands. Bright streaks showed on the metal scales of his brigandine, and his cloak was ripped in a dozen places.

He called, "Seyhat! To me with some men!"

"Trouble, Mark?" The lieutenant wiped blood from his cheek as he obeyed the command. A half-dozen mercenaries crowded behind him, grinning, eager to discover what loot the galley held.

"We must save those on the ship. Follow me!"

A dead man lay over a hatch. Carodyne kicked the body to one side and dropped through the hole into a shadowed dimness. A narrow walk stretched between benches holding the rowers for the oars. The stench was sickening. A man stared at him with dull eyes. He was emaciated, his back and shoulders scored with weals, a filthy rag covering his loins and festering sores on ankles and thighs. The other rowers were the same, dull, beaten and worked into an animal acceptance of a fate they could not avoid.

The romance of the sea, thought Carodyne sourly. The graceful galleys with their synchronized banks of oars which created white wings when in motion. A beautiful sight when seen from a safe distance—hell when you were chained to a bench.

To one of his men he said, "Open every hatch you can find. Let some light and air into here. Move!"

Seyhat touched his arm. "Mark?"

Carodyne ignored him. To the rowers he said, "This ship has been taken. Soon you all will be free. But first you must row to save others. Do you understand?"

They gaped at him with slack mouths, unable to appreciate the changed situation. One master was as bad as another. The whip stung just as much, the drum beat just as loud. They stirred a little as the hatches were flung wide,

89

resentful of the light which hurt eyes accustomed to dimness, the air which carried a cold chill.

Again Seyhat touched his arm. "...ark, they are beasts and fit only to work at the oars."

"They are men." Carodyne turned to his officer. "Find the drummer. Give the beat yourself if you cannot. We've got to rescue the others."

"How about the steering?"

"I'll stand by the prow and relay the course. We can steer by the oars until we clear the tiller."

Again on deck Carodyne looked to where the ship was foundering. From below the drum began to beat, slowly at first, quickening as the oars dug into the water. The galley had drifted a long way during the battle, the craft hard to get into motion. On the benches men sobbed as they strained against the thick timbers, the drum beating like a restless heart as the water was lashed into foam. Experience had turned the rowers into mindless machines and they obeyed the insistent beat, cringing to the expected lash.

"Faster!" ordered Carodyne. "Faster!"

Already the sea lapped over the edge of the sailing ship. In minutes the men clustered thick on the upperworks would be helpless before the circling sharks. Carodyne stood, weighing time and distance, judging the speed and position of the galley.

"Left-hand bank! Lift oars! Now!"

The blades lifted, hung suspended as the galley swung in a curve.

"Together! Now!"

The sinking ship came closer but still a little too far to one side.

"Right-hand bank back water! Now!"

It was clumsily done, but it was good enough. As the two hulls met with a dull crash men poured to the deck of the galley. Among the last was the captain. As the oars drove them away from the doomed vessel he came to where Carodyne was standing.

"The gods must have given you strength, my lord. You saved our lives."

Carodyne said, "Can you handle this ship? Take us to our destination?"

"With luck, yes. I have with me the magic of the sea." The captain opened his hand to show the scrap of wood and sliver of metal which had formed his crude compass. "A bowl of water and the charts I carry will enable me to plot a course. But I must warn you there will be danger. Galleys aren't suitable for deep waters. They are too narrow for their length. If we get caught by another storm we could be swamped."

"The alternative?"

Carodyne shrugged as the man hesitated. Obviously they could not head for the normal haunts of the galley. Equally obviously they couldn't stay where they were. And the man was pessimistic—on Earth ships manned with rowers had crossed oceans in time of presteam history. A storm was a chance they had to take. Another chance in this world where he seemed to be taking them all the time.

11

SMALL sounds echoed loud in the darkness, the rustle of a cloak, the tap of metal on metal, a soft curse as a stone turned beneath a boot. A man hawked and spat. Another tripped and almost fell, shingle rattling as he regained his balance. Carodyne turned and glared into the night.

"Tell those fools to be more careful. We could be walking into a trap."

He heard the soft mutter of relayed commands, Hostig's rumbled threats. Seyhat loomed abruptly at his side.

"I don't like this," he whispered. "Trapped between cliffs and the sea in a darkness fit only for the bowels of hell. Did the captain play us false?"

Carodyne doubted it. The man had seemed honest and had been open with his doubts. They were to the north of the agreed landing place but just how far north he hadn't been able to tell.

"We should be here, my lord," he'd said, a blunt finger resting on a promontory of land. "Cliffs edge the sea meeting the waves further to the north. They sweep westwards to join the city of Kedash, running south and then swinging to join the flanking mountains. The beach widens and, on it, the ships were to have landed."

But they had seen no ships, no fires, not the glimmer of a torch or beacon. Carodyne had decided to land and continue on foot. The galley had pulled out to sea.

He stumbled and regained his balance, water splashing from his boots. To his left he could hear the beat of surf, to his right nothing but an eerie emptiness, not even the flutter of seabirds taking wing as the column moved over the stoney beach.

A mile further and the darkness had thickened even more, closing around them like an inky fog. Carodyne halted and sniffed at the air. It held the tang of the sea, the odors of seaweed and brine, the scent of fish common to any ocean. He frowned, sniffing harder. There was something else, the faint but unmistakable scent of wood smoke. Drawing his sword he moved cautiously into the hampering darkness.

It grew almost solid and then began to thin, showing a dull glow, the embers of a smoking fire. Carodyne ran towards it, men following close behind. Before him other men rose from the ground, weapons lifted in belated defense. Hostig's voice roared in abrupt surprise.

"Nielagh! Carastes! Would you slay your friends?"

They had found the missing camp of the king.

Carodyne sheathed his sword as he neared the fire. Taut faces stared at him, hard and savage in the now-bright light of the flames. The faces of men who have fought and lost. Many were wounded, bound in crude bandages, blood dried on their clothing. A pot hung over the fire containing water in which floated scraps of leather and fragments of bird, fish and reptile. A thick scum covered the surface and the smell was vile.

Hostig stirred the pot with his sword. "Sheol! Is this all you have to offer hungry men?"

A soldier, his arm bound with bloodstained rags, stepped from the men assembled around the fire. "Offer? What makes you think you'll get any of this soup? Food is for those who've earned it—not laggards coming late to battle."

Hostig turned, his sword dripping slime. "The sea is in my ears, friend, and I would not willingly kill a wounded companion. But no man lives who calls me coward."

"If the helmet fits then wear it," snapped the man. "I've seen too much of death to be afraid of more. Strike if you want but I'll be no helpless dog to be butchered by your blade!"

Carodyne stepped between them as the soldier ripped out his sword. "Enough. We've no time for petty quarrels. Hostig, relax. He didn't mean what you thought."

"Then let him say so!"

"Maybe I spoke without thinking." Sullenly the soldier put away his sword. "But it isn't easy to see old comrades die for want of others to lend them strength."

"The delay wasn't of our choosing." Carodyne looked around the camp. "What happened? Where is the king?"

"Taken when we stormed the wall."

"And Albasar?"

"He lurks in his tent protected by magic." The man stared at Carodyne with a hopeful expression. "How did you get here? Have you a ship? Does it wait your return?"

"No," said Seyhat quickly. "We have no ship. We were wrecked far along the coast and made our way on foot. We have no food and no means of escape."

The hopeful expression vanished to be replaced by despair. "Then the gods aid us. Now we are all surely dead."

Albasar had set his tent hard against the foot of the cliff so that his back was protected by a wall of stone. He rose as Carodyne entered, tall and enigmatic in his silver-crusted robe, green eyes reflecting the light of a glowing gem. A small table was thick with ancient scrolls and a brazier threw up a thin thread of scented smoke.

"Mark! One prayer at least has been answered. I feared you had perished in the storm."

"We almost did."

"The king was convinced of it. Despite my advice he refused to wait for either you or your men. As you may have heard it was a bad decision. And you?" He listened as Carodyne told what had happened. "Your ship? Is it close?"

"Gone. I made a deal with the captain. Once we landed the ship was his to use as he wished. The slaves to be freed and the vessel sold. How about the others?"

"They also left. The captains refused to wait no matter what the king promised. Had the merchant brought us his wealth things would have been otherwise." Albasar shrugged. "Not that it would have made any difference. Now, at least, the men cannot escape. Had the ships remained they would be gone and you would never have found us."

"I almost didn't," said Carodyne. "The darkness around here is pretty thick."

"Marash grant that it continue to be so. I closed us in an ebon ring of fog to blind enemy eyes to our locale, but strong sorcery is hard close to the elemental forces of the sea. Yet it will suffice for the time." The sorcerer clapped his hands and to an answering slave said, "Bring us wine."

The man hesitated, "Master, it is the last."

"Then we shall enjoy it while we are able." Albasar handed Carodyne a goblet as the slave returned bearing an ewer of glazed earthenware. "We landed two days after embarkation, the men sick and in low spirits. A day we waited for you to join us and then the king would wait no longer. The country was scoured for aid, a few joining our standard, the majority running to the city or hiding beyond our reach. With the ships gone there was nothing else to do but attack."

"You could have retreated," said Carodyne. "Marched in a body and made your way to safety."

"So I told the king. My arts had shown that the omens were unfavorable and the time inauspicious, but he was on fire to win his throne. The walls of Kedash held him with a terrible fascination. He was convinced that, as soon as he attacked, those within the walls would rise and open the gates in happy welcome."

Carodyne frowned; Feya had not struck him as being a

complete fool. He said, "Was he influenced in any way? Mad perhaps?"

Albasar sighed. "I know what is in your mind. If he were afflicted by harmful demons why didn't I use my arts to cast them out? I tried. I read the stars and told him what I saw. But in some men there is a madness which has nothing to do with sorcery. No power can turn a man from his fated path. The king dreamed dreams based not on magic but on the desires of his heart. He chose to trust the friends he thought waiting behind the walls of the city. Those he thought trusted him and whom he could not betray. And so he made a gambler's throw."

"And lost."

"Even so." Albasar toyed with his goblet. "He lost as I knew he must, as I warned him he would. All day the battle raged. A dozen times we managed to scale the walls and each time the ladders were hurled back into the trench where men died from sting and fang. Twice we managed to cut a foothold on the ramparts before being beaten back. It was on the second such attempt the king was taken. They threw his surcoat and suit of mail from the walls as proof that he was in their hands."

Carodyne sat, leaning with his back against the cliff wall, frowning as he reviewed the situation. The wine was tart, bitter, but he drank it for the strength it contained. The last, the slave had said, and he remembered the pot of stew he had seen outside. A beaten army, now little more than a rabble, and he was caught among them. Like it or not their fate was his.

"For two days they have lived on scraps." The sorcerer had read his mind or expression. "We have no supplies."

"Then why not take what you need?" Carodyne finished the wine. "There are farms and fields, animals and grain in the land. There has to be in order to supply the city. Determined men have no need to go hungry."

"Determination isn't enough." Albasar unrolled a map. The city was picked out in golden threads, the mountains were woven of jet, the sea gleamed in silver. Red and green and blue traced boundaries, roads and fields. His finger rested on the curve of the mountains flanking the ocean.

"We are here. Between us and the approach to the city the beach narrows so that it is easily defended. Beyond the land spreads wide beneath the sun. If we leave this place riders from behind the walls will charge out to cut us down. To the north the mountains sweep down to the sea and are impossible to climb. Without ships we can't escape by water."

He paused, waiting for Carodyne to make a comment.

"We're in a trap."

"True. Iztima could send men against us, but for what purpose? All she has to do is to wait. Hunger will sap our strength and starvation kill as surely as a sword. Gold would buy the loyalty of the mercenaries—but why should she buy a victory which is already hers?"

Carodyne thought of the stinking mess within the pot.

"She wouldn't need money. The promise of food and safe-conduct would be enough. The men would accept such an offer."

Albasar was curt. "Some did. A herald came from the city bearing a flag of truce. To all who yielded their arms was promised meat and wine and a safe passage. I warned them of treachery but they wouldn't listen."

"And?"

"She kept her promise. Tables were set on the ramparts and we watched them feed. They ate and drank and called for us to join them. Had she waited another hour all would have responded, but she was impatient or the priests of Kanin eager for blood. As we watched she fulfilled the last part of her bargain. To each man was given a safe passage—to death."

Carodyne remembered the woman he had seen mirrored in the sorcerer's bowl. Could anyone so lovely be so cruel? He frowned, impatient with himself for clinging to familiar terms of reference. In this world beauty need have nothing to do with kindness. In fact there were few worlds where it did.

"They were thrown from the ramparts to hooks on the walls. Many took a long while to die. Some archers tried to end their misery and lost a half dozen of their number. The rest were eager to attack. If I had permitted them to have

96

their way all would have perished." Albasar leaned across the map. "Now, Mark, what do you suggest?"

Carodyne said, "We have little choice. Iztima must be made an offer. Either she employs us or we march across the land doing what damage we can. If she doesn't want to buy our service then she must give us supplies in return for leaving the land unmolested."

"She has horses," reminded the sorcerer. "Her riders could cut us to pieces."

"They could try," said Carodyne grimly. He knew how to beat a charge of mounted men. "There is driftwood on the beach and we have weapons. Sharpened stakes are a sure defense against cavalry if the men know how to use them. And we won't be a band of raiders searching for loot but an army under firm discipline. If she wise she will give us food and safe-conduct."

"And if not?"

"She must pay the price of her stupidity."

"To her it would be no price," said Albasar. "She wouldn't care what we did to the land and she wouldn't care how many men she lost to bring us down. Even if you could use your arts to defeat her horsemen we would have no hope. Men would rise from the ground against us driven by fear of the priests."

A pessimist, thought Carodyne, but the man was probably right. Guerrilla warfare would beat any army, especially one already at the limit of exhaustion, and if the woman didn't care about the cost sheer weight of numbers would beat them down. The alternative?

He sat, brooding, remembering lessons learned in the past. There were ways to take any fortification and he knew how a castle could be stormed. By towers with swinging bridges pushed close to send men to the upper ramparts. With sappers to pierce the defenses while protected by shielding mantles. With siege engines which would wear down and destroy by flinging masses of stone to breach the walls.

With cannon, lasers and high explosives, he thought bitterly. As well ask for one as the other.

He said, "If we could capture Iztima, hold her as a hostage, we could all get out of this with our lives."

"If men had wings they could fly," said Albasar dryly.

"They can."

"What?"

"Never mind." Carodyne rose. "How strong is your magic? Can you extend this darkness to the walls? Maintain it there so as to give us cover?"

The sorcerer hesitated. "The spells of the priests of Kanin are strong, but, yes, for a while at least I can do as you say. You have a plan?"

"I don't know," said Carodyne. "It depends on what I find when I reach the city."

12

THERE were drums, the thin wailing of pipes, the clash of cymbals and the throbbing clangor of gongs. The woman shrieked in wild abandon, her cries echoed with a burst of raucous laughter. Drifting from the high walls of Kedash the sound held a careless gaiety.

Seyhat glared at the invisible ramparts. "Listen to them," he snarled. "A city under siege and they loll at their pleasure. And yet why not? Who but a star-crossed fool would dream of doing a thing like this?"

Beyond him Hostig loomed from the thick darkness.

"The men are all in place," he rumbled. "Crouched in this trench of stone and shielded by magic from the vipers and scorpions. If they should wake we'll all be dead before dawn."

"By that time we'll be in the city or in no condition to worry."

Carodyne looked up to where the rounded turret of the city wall rose at the edge of the trench. Darkness cut off his vision a few feet above the ground, the flaring torches above hidden by the sorcerer's magic. He was stripped to pants, boots and lizard-skin shirt. A thin coil of rope hung over his shoulder, a thinner length weighed with a stone was looped over the pommel of his dagger. In his belt he carried a dozen more, thin-bladed things with wooden hilts. He thrust another between his teeth as he advanced to the wall.

"I'm coming with you," said Seyhat abruptly. "I climbed a lot when I was a boy."

Carodyne snarled around the blade of the dagger. "You'll stay with the others. Keep them alert and ready to act. Once I reach the top there'll be no time to waste."

He reached for the wall, digging the tips of his fingers into the cracks between the great blocks, lifting his weight as he searched for footholds. The wall was old, the mortar fallen from the joints in places; careless maintenance which had provided a crude ladder. Slowly he climbed, testing each hold before reaching for another. The magical darkness fell beneath him and he looked up at the dancing light of torches. They seemed very remote. A patch of lichen yielded beneath one hand and he tensed, clinging to the wall as he searched for a fresh grip. Again he felt ingrown moss beneath his fingers. Reaching higher he felt only smooth surfaces beneath the blocks of stone. Not all the mortar was old. Higher above the ground it had been renewed not too long ago.

Carodyne took the dagger from between his teeth and probed with the thin blade. It slipped into a fine crack and he hammered it deep with blows of his clenched fist. Gripping the hilt with his right hand he pulled himself upwards, boots scrabbling for the discarded handholds, left hand reaching for purchase. He found none and felt sweat break out on face and neck. Clinging grimly to the hilt of the dagger he pressed himself tight against the stone and reached out to the full extent of his left arm. He felt something, cautiously moved his left foot, felt it catch and then, abruptly, slip.

The jerk almost tore his hand from the dagger, and he felt the imbedded blade bend a little as he hung suspended by his right hand. Swinging up his left he changed his grip, found the remembered footholds and eased his weight as he again reached up the wall. This time he was lucky. A block had cracked in a jagged diagonal and he managed to dig his fingertips into the crevice. Cautiously he released his grip on the dagger, dragged himself upwards and rested his left boot on the hilt. His left hand found a hold and he paused to rest.

So far so good. He looked down and could see nothing in the somber darkness. From above came the thud of boots, the sound of a challenge followed by the murmur of voices. The sentries on their rounds, more interested in what was happening in the city than outside the walls. Carodyne hoped they would stay that way. Drawing in his breath he recommenced the climb.

Without the daggers it would have been impossible. Used as pitons they provided a secure hold for hand and boot, a defense against the wind which came gusting from the sea. He felt its tug as he crawled upwards, the pressure against his body as it threatened to tear him from the wall. He fought it as he moved like a spider up the turret, pausing as he reached the limit of the radiance cast by the flaring torches set behind the crenellations.

A dozen feet, he thought. Higher and he ran the danger of being seen by a guard on one of the other towers. It would have to do.

Finding a crack he drove in the last of the daggers, gripping it with his left hand, left boot hard against the hilt of another knife. With his right hand he loosened the thin length of weighted rope from where it hung over the pommel of his dagger. Letting a part slip through his fingers he began to swing the weight in a circle, widening it as he let out more rope. The stone made a soft humming noise as it cut through the air.

Curious, the sentry looked over the edge of the tower.

The rope swung, catching him on the side of the neck, the stone whipping around to throw a coiled noose about his throat. As it tightened Carodyne jerked with all his strength.

Soundless, like a dead bird, the sentry toppled over the edge.

Immediately Carodyne dropped the rope and swarmed up to the edge of the rampart. Cautiously he peered over the stone, saw the platform was deserted and threw himself over. Dropping the coil of rope from his shoulders he flung a loop over a crenellation and the rest over the parapet. Crouching, he waited, the slack of the rope in his hand. A tug and he pulled it upwards finding a heavier rope faste: ed to the end, his sword and brigandine, an axe and his helmet. Fastening the end of the heavy rope he donned helmet and brigandine, lifting the axe as he ran to where a door stood slightly ajar. Beyond it fell a spiral stairway. From below a door slammed and footsteps echoed as men began to climb up the stairs.

"Sorcerers!" A heavy voice snorted in disgust. "On a night like this when all are at festival we have to strengthen the guard. Free wine and willing women and I have to stand watch. And for why? Because some star-crazed sorcerer dreamed that rats were eating cheese. To hell with such omens!"

One of his companions laughed. "Never mind, Jeran. You would have got drunk and gambled away your pay. Think of what you are saving."

"By Kanin, that's small consolation." The heavy voice lifted. "Lorest! Is all well up there?"

Carodyne stepped softly away from the door. Resting a hand on the rope he found it taut with the weight of climbing men. To delay the guards would not be enough. A fight on the stairs would give the alarm and cost the invaders the advantage of surprise.

He looked around the platform. The door was set in a small tower topped by a conical roof which extended almost to the parapet and was designed to give protection from the weather. Cressets flared to either side, their light dancing in response to the gusting wind. In the flickering shadows the thin line of the rope was almost invisible.

To his left reared another watchtower beyond a length of curtain wall. In the light of its torches he could see a small knot of men, the increased guard milling as they talked. A shout would attract their attention and, again, the element of surprise would be lost. Ripping the torch facing them from its holder he threw it to the far side of the platform.

"Lorest!" The man with the heavy voice was almost at the door. "Answer, man! Is all well?"

Carodyne set down the axe and, drawing sword and dagger, pressed himself against the wall to one side of the door.

There would be three of them. The one with the heavy voice would arrive first, impatient, annoyed and careless because of that. He would slam open the door and rush onto the platform. His companion would follow close at his heels. The third man would be last and have time to become suspicious.

Therefore he had to be the first to go.

The door burst open and a thickset man rushed through the opening, a second at his back. Carodyne stepped forward as the third man appeared, his sword licking at the defenseless throat. Immediately he turned, steel whining as he slashed at the nape of the second man's neck, the edge biting deep between the base of the helmet and the neck of the hauberk. Warned by the whip of the blade Jeran turned. Carodyne threw the dagger as the man opened his mouth to shout the alarm.

He fell, coughing blood, the hilt rammed hard against his teeth.

"By all the gods I've never seen a shrewder throw!" Seyhat eased himself over the edge of the parapet. "Left-handed and smack in the gullet. Mark, never forget you are my friend."

He dropped a coil of rope as he spoke, another to add to the first. A horned helmet rose into view, Hostig grunting as he added another strand to those reaching below.

A voice called from the next watch platform.

"Ho there! Where is your light? Is all well?"

"Pass through the door and wait on the stairs," said Carodyne to the others and then, raising his voice, shouted at the curious guard. "All's well. The wind blew out the flame."

"Is that you, Lorest?"

"Kanin take you for a fool," yelled Carodyne heavily. "Can't you recognize the voice of Jeran?" He picked up the extinguished torch, relit it, held it before his face. "Well? Are you in love with my beauty that you stare so? Or are you afraid of the dark?"

Affronted the guard turned away. Carodyne thrust the torch back into its holder as men began to arrive from below.

The spiral stairway led down to a guardroom in which a handful of men sat with dice and wine. They died beneath a sudden flurry of naked steel. Blade dripping Hostig looked through a door then at Carodyne.

"It gives on the curtain wall. There are many men. Before we could silence them all the alarm would have been given."

"The stairs continue to the ground," said Seyhat thoughtfully. "If we assemble there we could take the gate."

It was good advice. Carodyne led the way down to the ground. They were lucky, the festival was in full swing and occupied everyone's attention. Soldiers, normally alert, were dreaming of pleasures lost or waiting when they were relieved.

Like ghosts they flitted along the base of the inner wall to where the great gate stood, locked, barred, guarded by a scatter of men.

Hostig's big hand clamped on the hilt of his sword. "Now?"

Delay was dangerous, but a plan was essential. Carodyne whispered at his officers.

"Hostig, you attack the far side of the gate. Seyhat, you take the near side. I'll hit the center and open the way. You cover me while I do it. We'll each take a third of the men. When the others get inside we'll all make straight for the palace and grab the queen." He tensed as a shout came from the ramparts. "Now!"

They hit the startled guards like a hurricane, steel biting deep, men dying before they knew what had hit them. Carodyne cut down an officer, dodged the sweep of a blade, sent his own edge to drink at a straining throat. Before him stood the barred mass of the inner portcullis. He yelled to his men and raced into the gatehouse where stood the great windlasses for gates and drawbridge. A savage flurry of vicious action and the place was his.

"Raise the portcullis!" he yelled. "Fast!"

Back in the arch of the gate he snarled his impatience as the thick grating slowly rose. Beyond stood great doors of oak crossed with metal straps, the locking bar chained and fastened with a huge padlock. Hostig came running, an axe in his hands, swinging it with all the massive strength of back and shoulders. Links burst before the hammering impact of the weapon. Grunting he threw it aside and joined Carodyne as he heaved at the massive panels. As they opened the drawbridge crashed down, the restraining ropes slashed by impatient swords.

103

From out of the darkness men came running.

They howled like wolves as they burst into the city, gaunt, starving, thirsting for revenge. Outnumbered, they had to hit and win before the defenders could get organized. To gain the palace, the queen, the only safety they could hope for.

Women screamed as they raced down the narrow streets, wild-eyed, weapons dripping blood. Men yelled and dived hastily into dwellings, slamming doors and shuttering windows. Others, unable to hide, ran before the attackers shrieking their fear. Garlanded revelers stared stupidly, befuddled with wine. Flaring torches threw a red light over banners of red and yellow, green and purple. All was noise, movement, battle and confusion.

Carodyne felt something strike against his helmet, something else kick at the tough scales of his brigandine. To one side a reveler screamed and fell, tearing at his stomach. A mercenary coughed as feathers sprouted from his throat.

Hostig roared a warning. "'Ware arrows! They have archers on the roof!"

Spiteful death bit among them, the danger passing as they burst from the narrow street and into a market. Stalls went crashing, bright fruits rolling underfoot, brassware and silks tumbling into the gutter. A woman shrieked as Carodyne grabbed her arm, her eyes wide with the fear of rape.

"The palace," he snapped. "Where is the palace?"

She gulped and lifted a hand. "Down that street. Turn left at the end and it'll face you across the square."

Carodyne ran in the pointed direction. The street curved, straightened as it met another crossing the end. From the left came a glow of light from massed torches set outside low buildings surrounding an open space. Revelers scattered as they burst from the street into a great plaza ringed with statues and gilded images. Before them loomed the great bulk of the palace and, as they watched, the great doors opened to release a massed phalanx of armored men.

They were tall, their height increased by crested helmets, wearing greaves, studded kilts and corselets of brass polished so that they shone like burnished gold. They carried oblong shields and, beside their swords, each man carried a ten-foot spear. As Carodyne led his men across the square they spread before the doors in a semicircular formation, lowering the heads of their spears so as to present a triple row of glittering points. Against such a firm-held barrier even charging horses would be helpless.

Seyhat grabbed Carodyne by the arm. "Slow down, man! What point in rushing forward to be skewered like a fish?"

Carodyne shook off the restraining hand. To slow now would be to create confusion and lose the impetus of the attack. Yet the lieutenant was right. The guards stood on a wide space before the door raised from the level of the square by a dozen broad steps. To make a frontal assault as they were would be to commit suicide.

"Iztima's personal guards," rumbled Hostig as he trotted beside the others. "They're the ones who threw our lads to the hooks." His voice became ugly. "Look at the gaudy sons of hell! Tonight they'll scream in torment!"

Carodyne glanced at the mercenaries loping behind. Already they had slowed a little, waiting for his lead. If he hesitated they would scatter, taking an easy revenge on the revelers, snatching loot and women until they were cut down by the organized defenses of the city. Yet how to defeat the spears?

He looked at the benches and tables lying where they had fallen when the feasting mob had fled. They were of thick wood and would make effective shields.

Hostig roared as he heard the plan. "By the gods, Mark! What demon gave you birth? You have the cunning of a snake!"

Slamming his sword into its scabbard the giant northerner picked up a twelve foot table. Lifting it above his head he yelled for others to follow his example. A bench in his hands, his sword between his teeth, Carodyne led the rush towards the waiting guards.

There was a way to break a barrier of spears. A horse couldn't do it, the animal would flinch from the stinging points, but men weren't beasts and had more than naked courage. Carodyne saw the gleam of points as he raced forward, the shine of metal above the edge of his crude shield, then he had mounted the steps and could see the taut faces beneath the rims of the crested helmets.

"Together!" he yelled. "Now!"

Without slackening his pace he slammed the bench lengthwise against the wall of threatening points, felt the jar as they dug into the wood and immediately heaved the bench upwards. He dropped, snatching the sword from between his teeth, cutting at the bare knees where they showed beneath the studded kilts, the edge scraping over the brazen greaves.

Fighting the weight of the bench stuck on their spears the men were helpless. Before they could drop the useless weapons and snatch at their swords Carodyne's blade had done its work. Crippled they fell to die beneath the thrust of his dagger.

Others of the phalanx followed, trapped by the unwieldy length of their spears, swords beating their sharp edges through brazen armor. Screaming their fury the mercenaries flung themselves forward, cutting, hacking, beating their way into the glittering mass. A snarling yell rose from the area, the sound of men who knew they had to win or die.

Carodyne ducked the swing of a glittering blade, felt himself pushed aside as Hostig lunged forward in fury, his broad blade whining as it cleared a bloody path. A man dropped, cursing as he tried to hamstring the northerner, slumping as Seyhat's rapier found his throat. Carodyne parried a slash, feinted and sent his point deep into an exposed armpit. A guard cut viciously at his head, missed, scored a path over the brigandine. He lifted his sword to cut again and died as Carodyne sent his dagger crashing through an eye into the brain beneath.

The battle was taking too long. Carodyne sprang clear, shook sweat from his eyes and yelled to his officers. "Hostig! Seyhat! Get men and follow me!"

He ran through the open door of the palace, the need for speed a driving urgency in his blood. Behind him came the thud of feet, Hostig's bull-like roar.

"Mark! Wait!"

A broad chamber opened beyond the door, the floor tessellated with triangles of silver and jet. Columns rose to either side of the slender pillars bearing great flambeaux which threw a flood of ruby light. From behind the pillars stepped armed and armored men.

106

"A trap!" Hostig's voice echoed from the vaulted roof of the chamber. "Mark! Seyhat! To me!"

He turned and flung himself towards the open portal beyond which men still fought. He hit something invisible, cursed and tried again. Snarling he beat at the barrier with his sword.

"Sorcery! By all the gods of hell what manner of magic is this?" Eyes blazing he glared at the closing ring of guards. "Well, if this is death I shall not die alone!"

Seyhat's rapier whispered through the air as he stepped beside Carodyne. "Three of us," he said grimly. "Well, the odds could be better, but they are not so great. Do we wait or attack?"

Carodyne watched the approaching men. They were cautious, reluctant to engage and, perhaps, to die. A natural fear which could be exploited by desperate men. If they could break through the ring, head into the palace and take a hostage or two, they might even yet have a chance.

He said, "We attack. When I give the word make for the end of the chamber. If we see stairs head for them. Take anyone who looks important alive. Ready?"

"Ready," whispered Seyhat, and Hostig's rumble echoed the word.

"Now!"

They burst through the guards like a storm, sword and dagger leaving dead and wounded sprawled on the tessellated floor, the sound of their boots loud as they raced down the chamber. Ahead of them more guards appeared this time armed with crossbows, stocks to shoulder, the light of the flambeaux turning the heads of the quarrels into points of crimson fire. Carodyne threw himself towards the shelter of the pillars, hearing the thrum of strings, the vicious hiss of missiles. Stone splintered before his eyes and something rang sharply on his helmet, then he was down, rolling, his mouth dry with anticipated death.

If the men were disciplined only half of them would have fired, the others withholding their quarrels for a second volley. With the approaching swordsmen to hold them in check they would be helpless targets. But the volley did not come. Instead he heard the sharp snap of a command.

107

"Hold!"

An officer stood behind the ring of bowmen, a woman at his side. Regaining his feet Carodyne met her eyes.

"Move and you die!" snapped the officer.

Carodyne ignored him, looking at the woman. She was tall, her hair a golden cascade over her rounded shoulders, cloth of silver taut against the supple curves of her body. He recognized her at once. Iztima, ruler of the city, the prize he had hoped to take.

Would take if he could cut his way through the ring of guards. Once he had her fast, his dagger to her throat, the way would be open to leave the city.

She said, "I would not try it. Move a single step and all three of you will die. My men will not miss a second time."

Perhaps not, but desperate men had nothing to lose and it took time to aim and fire. As Carodyne tensed his muscles for explosive action the woman lifted her hands.

"You are brave," she said, "but foolish. If my men cannot bind you then my magic can."

Carodyne saw the slender hands weave in a peculiar pattern and felt the touch of a stinging numbness. He tried to take a step forward and found he could not force his muscles to obey. Beside him he heard Seyhat's indrawn breath.

"Gods, I cannot move! The witch has us in her power!"

Hostig's rumble held a helpless terror. "My arms! What spell is this that robs a man of his strength?"

She smiled, her voice like the chiming of bells. "Taneft! It is time the city was cleared of vermin. See to it!"

A squat figure stepped beside her. He wore a robe of woven metal glimmering with costly gems. A cap of brilliant feathers crowned a seamed and arrogant face, the plumage surmounted by a disc of featureless jet. He raised both arms and moved them on a complex pattern of involuted symbols. A harsh sound came from between his thin lips, syllables which seemed to dim the light of the flambeaux and twist the lines of the chamber into disturbing proportions.

A gelid cold passed over Carodyne. He felt the frigid touch of it, then it left him to flow towards the portal and the area beyond.

The squat man lowered his arms, eyes blazing with a savage pleasure. "It is done, my lady," and then, to Carodyne, "Behold the power of Kanin!"

Carodyne found he could move a little. Outside the palace, heaped together in an untidy mass, the mercenaries and defending guards lay slumped in the stillness of death. A thick white frost covered them as if with a shroud.

"You are defeated," said the woman. "Your foolish attack on my city has failed and all your men are dead other than those who stand beside you. And soon, you too will die. Think of it while you wait!"

13

THERE was a smell of sweat, smoke and urine. Carodyne rose from a litter of filthy straw and crossed the cell to where thick bars rose from floor to roof. Beyond he could see an open area containing a rough table bearing an urn and cups of baked clay. A bench stood beside the table. Burning wicks floating in containers of rancid oil provided a dim illumination. By its light he could see a cage fastened high against one wall. In it a man threshed and whimpered in ceaseless torment.

A nice place, thought Carodyne grimly. Like the others he had been stripped naked before being thrown into the cell, but, while they slept, he had sat, brooding. The display of magic had startled him. Until now he had thought that sorcery had been a matter of different terminology, but obviously it was more than that. A control of natural forces by means other than those he had known, perhaps. Or maybe the laws of this world were not the same as in his own universe. Spells and incantations which really worked. Gods which were more than names or carved idols.

A force screen could have sealed the door to the palace. A numbing dust could have induced the paralysis, but what had caused the extreme cold? Absolute zero would have frozen the men, that or a deluge of some liquid gas, helium, for example, but the squat man had used no apparatus other than his arms and voice. Another attribute of the Omphalos, he thought bleakly. How many more remained to be discovered?

Irritation drove him back to the bars. They were firmly set in the stone. The lock was crude but impossible to open without instruments.

Hostig woke, roaring, slamming his fist viciously into the straw. A scuttling thing squelched beneath his knuckles. Picking it up he flung it through the bars.

"Curse the thing! I was dreaming of a loaded table and wine served by a smiling wench when that creature from hell decided to drink my blood. Well, it will drink no more."

Seyhat stirred, his dark eyes glistening with ironic amusement. "Would you who are so large begrudge a meal to a thing so small?"

"Aye, large or small it is all the same. I don't like to make a meal for others." The big northerner laughed as Seyhat swore and slapped at his leg. "But you, comrade? Surely you are more generous?"

"Sheol take this stinking place!" Seyhat rose, kicking at the straw. "Better to have died cleanly in the open than rot here waiting until that witch determines how painfully she can kill us. How about the lock, Mark? Can it be picked?"

"No."

Hostig rose, scars white on the barrel of his chest. "We should be making plans. Unless they intend for us to die in here they will bring food and water. When they open the door we will attack."

"If they open the door," corrected Seyhat. "Most likely they will thrust what they bring through the bars."

"Then we will catch their arms, draw them close and threaten immediate death unless they open the door." Hostig paced the cell like a trapped beast. "If they kill us what does it matter? Better to die than to linger in agony like that poor devil in the cage."

A door slammed somewhere to the left. Light shone redly from torches held in the mailed fists of armed and armored guards. They separated, standing against the far wall as others leveled spears at the three men in the cell, the points stabbing between the bars. Hostig cursed as one drew blood from his chest. Grabbing the shaft he stepped aside and jerked. The guard slammed heavily against the bars but retained his grip on the weapon. His companions knew their business. Immediately they thrust their points at the northerner's face, forcing him to release his grip and jump back in order to save his eyes.

"Neatly done," murmured Seyhat. "And it seems we have company."

A voice barked a command and the guards withdrew their weapons, backing so as to leave a clear space before the cell. Into it stepped Albasar.

The sorcerer was as impassive as ever, still wearing his jewels, his embroidered robe of black and silver, but his face showed signs of strain. Gaudy in his feathered headdress, Taneft stepped to his side.

"Here you will wait, sorcerer. See what power Marash has to save you now."

"Power enough, perhaps," said Albasar quietly. "Enjoy life while you may, Taneft. Even the High Priest of Kanin cannot escape his fate and the vengeance the future will bring."

"You talk like a fool. Misapplied spells have muddled your brain. Enter and wait what is to come!"

Regal in his dignity the sorcerer entered the cell, remaining immobile as the door slammed shut behind him, the guards tramping away. Only when the unseen door closed with a muted thunder of rolling echoes did he relax.

"We meet again in an evil hour," he said. "May Marash guard us from further harm."

"They caught you," said Hostig. "But how? Your sorcery—"

"Was not strong enough to protect me from the vile priests of Kanin." Albasar leaned tiredly against a wall. "Their god must be very close for them to have such power. I had wrapped myself in darkness together with spells of invisibility proof against all normal magic, but it was as if I had stood naked in the bright light of day." He looked at the three men. "The others?"

"Dead." Seyhat scraped his naked foot in the straw. "Slain by a blast of freezing cold."

"I saw it," admitted the sorcerer, "but I had hoped more had survived. Yet perhaps they have not died in vain. Great spells demand great payment and Kanin is a greedy and a cunning god. It could be that the score will rise higher than the priests are willing to pay."

Carodyne frowned, not understanding, then said, "Can't your sorcery get us out of this cell?"

"No. The bars are of iron sealed with protective spells of great power."

Nothing to do then but wait. Carodyne sat, leaning his back against a wall, trying to ignore the whimpering of the man in the cage. A sample of the cruelty of the queen, he thought grimly. A foretaste, perhaps, of what was to come.

Seyhat said, casually, "A beautiful woman, our captor. How could one so lovely be so vile?"

"She must be possessed," rumbled Hostig. "A black demon has taken over her mind and body using them as instruments of darkness. When we find such in the north we purge them with fire."

Carodyne looked at the sorcerer. "Is that possible? You knew her when she was young, was she always as she is now?"

"No," admitted Albasar. He paused, thinking. "When she was very young she was as sweet as a flower. In those days Marash was worshiped in the temple and Kanin was a minor god worshiped in dark places. The old king died and Feya took his place. Shortly afterwards Iztima seemed to change. The cult of Kanin grew in power, intrigue sundered the court, rebellion swept Feya from his throne and Iztima ruled in his place. Marash was ousted from the temple and the altar of Kanin replaced the flame of purity."

"History," said Carodyne. "But did anything else happen at the time? Before the rebellion, I mean, or about that period?"

Albasar shrugged. "I had my duties to Marash and could not be aware of all the small events of the court. Also the new king needed my counsel and the use of my powers to protect the land. Later, when I attempted to search the past, I found it occluded by nighted barriers of sorcerous darkness."

"And the future?"

"Only the gods can be certain of what is to come, but I will venture a prophecy." Albasar's eyes shone like emeralds as he looked at Carodyne. "The guards will come to take you to Iztima within the space of five hundred beatings of your heart."

She stood in a chamber all of onyx and ivory, inlaid tables scattered on furred rugs bearing statuettes, vases, things of price. Her hair rose in a golden cloud of plaited tresses, the thick coils bound with silver. More silver threaded the scarlet robe which hugged the contours of her body, a silver belt cinching the narrow waist, more silver meshed in sandals hugging her delicate feet. A great ruby glowed from the index finger of her left hand.

"Your majesty!" The captain of the guards which had collected Carodyne from the dungeon bowed with exaggerated deference. "The prisoner as you ordered."

The ruby glittered as she lifted her hand. "Leave us."

As the officer backed away Iztima stepped closer to Carodyne, her eyes coolly appraising. He had been washed, his hair dressed, his body covered with a robe of watered silk. About him hung an odor of perfumed waters.

"You are tense," said the woman. Her voice was as soft and sweet as the chiming of bells. "Wary and wondering what is going to happen to you. That is natural and, in a way, your future depends on yourself. But know this. If you lift your hand against me you will fall in torment. Would you care to put the matter to the test?"

Later, perhaps, he might, but not yet, not now when she was fully prepared. He remained silent, watching as she poured wine into goblets of emerald glass, taking the one she offered.

"Have you no fear of poison?"

"If you wanted me dead," said Carodyne bluntly, "there would be no need of wine."

"True, and you are shrewd to realize it. Or perhaps you had another reason," she mused. "I have, in a sense, given you a weapon. Wine to throw into my eyes, a goblet to shatter and hold at my throat. Or maybe you hadn't thought of that?"

He shrugged and sipped at the wine. It was cloyingly sweet and held the tang of burning spices. It lit a fire in his stomach, warming him with an increased awareness of the woman's femininity. He tilted the goblet, pretending to drink but swallowing nothing.

"You trust me," she said. "That is good. I feel that we have much in common. You are tall and brave and far from being the mercenary you seem. Taneft says that you contain the seeds of great powers and that I can well believe. No ordinary man could have penetrated the walls of my city. Tell me, why did you fight against me?"

"I had no choice. It was fight or die."

"And so you fought." Her voice deepened a little. "As you were born to fight. Isn't that right, Mark? You see, I know your name. Mark Carodyne who comes from who knows where? And when you first saw me, Mark, what did you think?"

He said, honestly, "I thought you were very beautiful."

"And kind?" She shrugged as he made no answer. "Men do not sing of my kindness, Mark. Neither do they say I am gentle. They say that I am cruel but, in this world, what woman can afford to be weak? I rule, yes, but at what a price none can guess. I am alone. In all this land there is none that I dare trust, none that I dare to love—and I am a woman with a woman's need."

A barbarian, he thought, a creature of emotive impulse yielding to a whim. Or was it more than that? She was a woman, lovely it was true, but with a hint of something in her eyes he could not trust. Mockery, perhaps, or sadistic anticipation. Her offer, the intimacy of the room, all could be the bait of a savage trap. Yet he had no choice but to play along.

Smiling he said, "My lady, you are the most attractive woman I have seen. You do more than rule Kedash. You rule the hearts of every man who sees you. There is no need for you to be alone."

Her goblet rang as she set it down, a thin, high note of

absolute purity. "Your words please me, Mark. I would hear more."

He followed her to a couch on which she sat, all red and silver, the glinting threads reminding him of a web. A spider toying with her mate, to use him and, afterwards, to destroy him. To laugh, perhaps, as she did so. He sat, remembering the cell, the man threshing in his cage. No matter how she looked there was vileness in her, a cruelty all the more repugnant because she looked so fair.

She said, "Life is hard, Mark, the more so when you rule and even more when you are a woman alone. But now that the false king is dead I can spare thought for the future."

"Feya? Dead?"

"Alive he was a constant source of irritation, a focal point for every rebellious subject and ambitious noble. Now he can be forgotten." She moved a little closer so that he could smell the scent of her perfume. "Can you appreciate my problem, Mark? Who in all Kedash dare I trust to share my throne? Who, outside the walls, would be fit enough to remain at my side? Obey me and your future is assured."

Quietly he said, "As your husband or as your slave?"

"If you loved me would it matter?"

"It matters. A man must have his pride."

"A cockerel who struts and crows and boasts of his conquest? Mark, you disappoint me."

A game, he thought dispassionately, one in which he held no cards even though his life was at stake. To win he had to cater to the whims of a sadistic girl.

"You must not blame me for being ambitious," he said. "But to serve you would be reward enough."

She smiled and reaching out touched his hand, her slender fingers running over his knuckles, his wrist. Boldly he returned the caress, stroking the silken texture of her hair. She yielded, turning, her lips moist, teeth white between the parted lips. His free hand lifted towards her throat, the carotid arteries which could be pressed to bring unconsciousness and death. A moment and she would be utterly helpless in his arms.

"Fool!" She reared back, her left hand slashing at his face,

115

the ring on her finger catching his nose and filling his eyes with water. "Did you think to conquer me so easily?"

He blinked, too startled to answer. Where should have sat a young and lovely woman crouched a withered crone. A scrap of white hair clung to a yellowed skull. Toothless jaws gaped in a parody of a smile. The face was taut with parchment skin stretched over prominent bone.

Savagely he shook his head, clearing his eyes of moisture, and, abruptly, the crone had vanished and Iztima sat in her place. Her hand lifted and he was unable to move.

"The crone." His throat ached as he forced out the words. "You were an old woman."

"You know," she said. "I saw it in your eyes. Then know even more. I am Mukalash, favored of the gods! I have a sorcery so great that I summoned a being from outer darkness. Together we made a pact. In return for my opening the path I was promised anything I desired. I chose this!" She slapped her hand against her thigh.

"A new body," said Carodyne painfully. "Now I begin to understand."

"I was born to a hill farmer and lacked the favor of men," she continued more quietly. "Famine came and I was sold as a slave. A magician bought me as a household drudge and, unknowing to him, I studied his books and learned many secrets. When he died I gained my freedom. By magical arts I managed to enter the household of the rulers of Kedash. The old king used me first as nurse then as governess to his daughter. Can you imagine the hell in which I lived?"

Iztima rose and stretched, the light from glowing gems shimmering from the lustrous pile of her hair.

"The chit was fair and favored of all. I was old and ugly and heeded by none. In despair I deepened my knowledge of sorcerous arts, venturing into realms which would have blasted the mind of a lesser being. In a space between dimensions I met the one men know as Kanin. It was with it I made my bargain and we have both kept it to the letter."

"You gave it priests," said Carodyne. "A temple and the homage of a city. And it gave you a new body in return."

"This body. I left my old and whithered shell and entered this container. The girl struggled and struggles still but to no avail. She watches as I turn her city into a place of blood and pain. And why not? For too long they despised the old governess and, despite her smiles and protestations of affection, she hated me as much as the rest. Now I rule and will do as I choose until this body grows old and I leave it to inhabit another. Bodies without end for time without end. Always shall I live and always shall I rule."

Carodyne said, thickly, "And me?"

The woman smiled and beat a gong. To the guard who answered the summons she said, "Summon men. Inform the High Priest that he is to prepare for an offering. We have a sacrifice for Kanin."

14

SOMEWHERE a man was whimpering, "Oh, god! Oh, dear, sweet god! Oh gentle Marash save me from my enemies! Oh merciful—"

"Shut your whining mouth!" the voice was deep, harsh with impatient anger. "Talk sense or I'll give you something to whine about!"

"No! Oh dear god let him not—" The whimper broke off, turned into a scream. "No!"

There was a sharp hiss. The scream rose, echoing from the roof of the dungeon, then died in a falling moan. The deep voice snarled a curse.

"Kanin take these merchants! A touch of hot iron and they faint like children. Jemba! Wake him with water and give him the bastinado. I'll find out where he has hidden his jewels if I have to flay him inch by inch."

An eager voice rose above the splash of water.

"Master, I've heard of a persuasion much used in the land

of Keemel. Splinters of wood are thrust deep beneath the fingernails and then set on fire. May I use that means of loosening his tongue?"

Rumbling laughter echoed from the vaulted roof. "Kanin take me for a sacrifice! You show the true spirit, young Jemba. Use what means you will but don't kill him. Learn his secret and I'll buy you a new jerkin." Heavy footsteps thudded on the floor.

Carodyne jerked to a sudden deluge of water.

Shaking his head he opened his eyes. The torturer stood before him, wide-legged, his leather jerkin old and stained with dirt and blood. Piggish eyes stared from under bushy brows and the naked skin of his scalp showed red in the light of flambeaux. A matted beard parted to show rotting teeth.

"So you sleep, my pigeon. Are you so eager to taste the nothingness which awaits?"

Carodyne hadn't been asleep. He had relaxed against the wall, arms and legs held with chains, conserving his energy for what was to come. Beyond the tormentor, through an open door, he could see the loom of monstrous implements, the rack, pulley, the iron horse and maiden, the glowing brazier in which rested rods and twists of iron. A shadow moved and the unseen victim shrieked in agony.

"Dear god! No! No! My hands!"

Jemba's youthful treble rose, shrill with excitement. "Where are your jewels? Tell me where you have hidden them and I'll stop the torment. Talk, old man, or—" The thin voice broke into a stream of petulant curses. "By the gods! Again he has fainted!"

The tormentor shook his head. "The lad is too eager. He has yet to learn the art of patience. Secrets are not easily wrung from those who are stubborn. Yet, give him a few more years under my direction, and he will wring conversation from the very stones."

"I doubt it," said Carodyne. "He lacks finesse."

The tormentor blinked.

"There are other ways of making men talk," said Carodyne. "And you don't have to rip apart their flesh to do it. You people have a lot to learn."

"Magic?" The tormentor shrugged. "It won't work down

here. There's too much iron about for a spell to take hold. It's been tried."

"Not magic," said Carodyne. "Psychology and nervous attrition. Give me time and I'll make him tell you everything he knows. More, he'll be begging to tell you—and I won't leave a mark on him."

"Is that so?" The man prodded at one of his teeth. "How would you do it? Look," he urged, as Carodyne made no answer. "I'm always willing to learn. Tell me the secret and I'll ease your chains a little. Give you some wine too, maybe. Is it a deal?"

"Take the chains off and I'll think about it."

"You know I can't do that. They'll be coming for you any moment now and if they see you free I'll be in trouble. But I can manage the wine."

"Make it water," said Carodyne. "Water with a little salt in it."

He eased his muscles as the man moved away. The bonds were tight but bearable, and he'd known better than to struggle. Time, it seemed, was needed for the sacrifice to be arranged, but he wished it could have been spent in more comfortable surroundings.

He looked up as men came from the room beyond. An officer wearing the crested helmet and brazen armor of Iztima's personal guard thrust his way to where Carodyne stood. Their eyes met as he loosened the bonds.

"My cousin died beneath your sword," he muttered. "I pray that you might suffer an eternity of pain."

Carodyne stretched. The officer stood too close and could be killed or maimed with a blow, but his men were watchful and escape was impossible. Quietly he allowed himself to be led from the chamber, through the outer room where the torturer stood with a cup of water, to a flight of stairs leading to the upper levels.

Taneft stood waiting in a circle of acolytes and priests.

"You have a choice," he said curtly. "You can walk as a man or be dragged like a beast. Struggle or attempt to escape and the latter will happen. If you have pride and dignity you will walk as a man."

A lamb to the slaughter, thought Carodyne, but again he

119

had no choice. The odds were against him and it was futile to get himself beaten and injured. Later, if there was a chance, he would take it.

Light blazed as they passed through a door, the glow of massed torches, the flare of cressets and flambeaux. Dazzled he could see a double line of devotees all wearing gaudy plumes, each bearing the symbol of featureless jet which was the disc of Kanin. In their midst he moved forward as trumpets blared, the echoing notes mingling with the rattle of sistrums, the brazen throb of gongs. Drums caught at the senses, inducing hysteria with their relentless pounding. Like a brightly colored, gem-encrusted serpent the procession wended across the annex towards the inner precincts of the temple.

A great chamber opened beyond the valves of a huge door. The columns supporting the vaulted roof were plated with electrum, the roof itself studded with a mass of gems. Incense rose in thick clouds and filled the air with a heady perfume. Voices rose in a sonorous chant as they moved between serried ranks of worshipers. At the far end the marchers split to either side so that Carodyne was pressed forward to stand alone before the altar.

He studied it as the High Priest mounted the dais.

A great slab of stone, probably obsidian, polished to a mirror brightness rested on the low platform. Above and beyond it, facing the great hall, reared a featureless disc of ebon darkness fully twenty feet in diameter. It was surrounded by a ring of gilded metal which reflected the light in shimmers of dancing brilliance. But there was no reflection from the disc itself. The dark surface seemed to absorb all light as if it were a sponge.

Taneft faced the disc, made obeisance, rose with his arms flung wide. A gong throbbed and, as the echoes died, he lifted his voice.

"Oh great Kanin, Destroyer of Worlds, Ruler of Darkness, Giver of Power, Keeper of the Gate, we pay you homage!"

Again the throb of the gong.

"To you, great Kanin, we kneel in humble adoration!"

Now, thought Carodyne as he heard the rustle from the congregation. He turned and saw the glinting points of a ring of spears. The guards had not knelt. They stood, faces tense, scared almost, facing both him and the disc. He glanced to either side. More guards, more spears, a double row to left and right.

Forward then, up and over the altar, a spring to the disc and beyond where there could well be a door. If he could reach it, get through it, there might be a chance.

Carodyne tensed as the gong throbbed a third time. Taneft moved from before the disc as men came forward bearing straps. One doubled, retching as Carodyne slashed the stiffened edge of his hand across the naked throat, another screamed as his foot found the groin, a third reeled backwards hands to his face, blood streaming from between his fingers. Before the others could reach him Carodyne leaped onto the altar.

And froze.

Something watched him from the ebon disc. It was a formless swirling, black on blackness, the impression of eyes, of jaws which champed in insectlike ferocity, a thing of mind-numbing horror all the more terrible because of its very vagueness. A creature of slime and delirious nightmare, a vileness spawned in the darkest pits of fevered imagination.

Taneft's voice rose, screaming.

"To you, great Kanin, we offer this sacrifice! To you this gift of blood! Hearken to us when we pray!"

It had come too soon, thought Carodyne. Had been too eager to feed. It should have waited until he had been firmly strapped to the altar, but he was free to fight and run and, perhaps, to escape.

He turned and saw the spears, the terrified faces of the men behind the glittering points, others running with crossbows. He looked again at the disc. From it came probing tentacles, broad-tipped, writhing, suckered and coated with a slimy ooze. They quested the air, lengthening, hungry.

Votive offerings stood to either side of the dais, tripods, urns, goblets, things of price. Among them gleamed the gemmed hilt of a sword. Carodyne sprang towards it, raised it high as a tentacle clamped around his waist. The blade whined through the air as he chopped down, the edge biting into a rubbery surface, green ichor flowing from the gaping wound. Again he slashed, drawing back the edge as it struck. The tentacle fell away as two others gripped his legs and free arm. Struggling furiously he was drawn towards the ebon disc.

From it came a thick slobbering, the gusting sigh of a gelid wind.

Light gleamed from the metal surround. Carodyne caught at it with his left hand and stabbed the point of his sword at the surface of the disc. It was though he thrust at smoke. The tentacles gripping him tightened and, with a savage jerk, tore his grip from the metal. He caught a glimpse of the guards, the worshipers, the face of the High Priest, and then all was darkness.

It was thick, clammy, pressing on eyes and skin as if a liquid. He felt the constriction on arms and legs, the hilt of the sword in his hand, the flexing of his muscles as he slashed blindly all round. A gust of frigid air numbed him with sudden cold. Something rough and spined rasped against his thigh. He chopped, felt resistance, slashed again. The grip of the tentacles eased a little, and he writhed as he maintained his attack.

Abruptly he was free, falling, spinning as he fell, the wind droning around him and then rising to a thin keening which faded in turn. Silence joined the darkness as he tumbled through unimaginable distance. Wings of softness closed around him, carried him to one side and set him down on a surface which felt as if composed of rubble and spines. He tripped, fell, managed to stand upright on a pulsating substance. He fell again and realized that he was being moved in a certain direction. Dropping on all fours he crawled over what seemed to be a warted hummock.

Reaching out he felt softness and drove the blade of his sword into something which felt like jelly. He stabbed again, twisting the weapon and feeling a gush of wetness slime his hand and arm.

A scream of rage echoed in his skull.

Beneath his feet the surface twitched and again he was falling through endless darkness. The darkness changed into a pearly luminescence which condensed into points of brightness against which moved a tremendous scorpion. The brightness grew into a sparkling flood of light. Beneath him stretched a landscape of nightmare proportions.

A bowl of sand which faced a sky of emerald flame. Trees which reared a thousand feet. Flowers as large as palaces, boulders as big as houses, droplets glinting like polished lakes. A silver web into which he fell. A spider as large as a hundred-oared galley. It advanced, eyes like gems, mandibles gnashing in eagerness to suck the juice from its prey.

The sword whined, muscles forcing the dull edge through hampering strands, chopping away the snare which held him fast. The blade shone like burnished gold as Carodyne raised it high, brought it down in savage arcs. Chitin yielded beneath its impact, ichor gushing from the stumps of severed limbs, welling from the ripped abdomen, the hacked mandibles. Dropping from the web Carodyne raced across the sand and watched as the spider died.

It grew smaller as he watched, smaller, the flowers shrinking, the trees becoming grass.

From above came the sound of tearing cloth.

Carodyne looked at the sky. It opened and a claw reached down, gripped him, flung him into space. A grotesque creature hanging from an inflated bladder caught him as he passed, the touch of its whiplike tendrils searing like acid. Ignoring the pain Carodyne clamped the sword between his teeth, gripped the thin strands and began to climb. He saw goggling eyes, a wizened face, the great dome of the bladder above. Gas hissed free as he ripped it open with the point of the sword. Together they fell towards a sea edged with drifting clouds of colored smoke.

Releasing his hold on the creature, Carodyne plunged beneath the waves. He surfaced, gasping, aware of imminent danger. A ripple cut towards him and he dived, seeing gaping jaws and a yellow body arrowing through the water. He swam to one side and thrust as the creature passed. Blood fogged the ocean as he surfaced, gasping. The smoke shifted and he saw the shore. A man stood watching as Carodyne crawled from the sea.

"You will never be able to survive," he said. "Why do you bother to struggle against forces so powerful?"

Carodyne shook water from his hair and rose to his feet

looking at the stranger. He was an old man, white of hair and beard, wearing a simple robe of brown fabric tied at the waist with a knotted cord. His feet were bare. He shook his head at Carodyne's silence.

"Kanin is too powerful for you to resist. Why not let yourself be assimilated into the essence of his being? This struggle is futile. How can you, a mortal man, hope to defeat a god? The concept is ridiculous. Gods cannot be defeated. Throw away that foolish weapon and accept your destiny."

"It may be true that a god cannot be destroyed," said Carodyne. "But who says that Kanin is any such thing?"

"Kanin is worshiped."

"So are many other things and not one of them is more than it seems. Love, for example, money, power over others. Authority, command, learning. In any case it is not my nature to yield to destruction."

"Assimilation is not destruction. Enter willingly into the essence of Kanin and you will live forever. You will become part of the god and be given great power." The old man held out his hand. "Now come, stop being so stupid. Give me that sword."

Carodyne slashed at his neck.

Dull though the blade was, the force he put into the blow was enough to send the head leaping from the shoulders. It rolled on the ground, eyes still wide. Calmly the old man picked it up and held it in his arms.

"Do not make the mistake of thinking this is a dream," he said. "You fight the manifestation of a power greater than you can guess."

"A scavenger," said Carodyne. "A thing which lurks behind an interdimensional gate in order to feed on the unwary."

"Perhaps. Even so you are powerless before it. Beware the revenge which awaits!"

Colored smoke drifted around the headless figure and, when it cleared, the figure was gone.

Grimly Carodyne looked around. He was caught between dimensions at the mercy of whatever life forms inhabited the region. Here, obviously, the one known as Kanin was dominant. An amorphous entity which adopted many forms and used different forms of attack. And yet it seemed afraid of his sword. He studied it, seeing the runes engraved on the blade, mystic symbols which could hold an unsuspected power. A pattern which served to disturb the atomic balance of the creature, perhaps. A relationship of lines and angles, curves and arcs which would act on the thing as, perhaps, an irritant poison would on a man. Not fatal, not even serious, but just inconvenient.

A scrap of sorcery which had saved his life.

But for how long?

Abruptly the light changed, the swirling clouds of mist congealing into shapes of vague familiarity. The air opened like a door to reveal crystalline formations stooped in awkward obeisance before a disc of ebon darkness. The image changed to show tall figures like mobile trees rubbing wooden arms together as a stunted bush shriveled before another of the hateful discs. Icicles, bees, things of gossamer, birds with brilliant plumage, dull mounds of pulsating jelly, life in a dozen forms and all worshiping at the blank circle of the interdimensional gate.

A voice whispered in his mind.

"Behold the power of Kanin."

"All right," yelled Carodyne. "So you're big and strong and figure you can't be beaten. Well, why not put it to the test? A gamble. You win and I throw away the sword. I win and you let me go. Agreed?"

"A gamble?"

"Chance. If you are so powerful you can't lose. Fate will work on your behalf." He picked up a stone, spat on it, rotated it in his hand so as to wet both sides. "Wet side up I win. Dry and you can take me. Here goes!"

He tossed the stone.

It was raw, too elementary to have a hope, and yet it was all he could do. And a thing so powerful might not be aware of the small tricks men played on each other. It might not know how to cheat. If it did not then Carodyne was certain to win.

The stone fell. There was a pause and then a gelid wind roared from the sea. It picked up Carodyne as if he had been a leaf and sent him whirling through endless regions of interdimensional space. He saw the glazing fury of suns, the awful majesty of distant stars, heard the mind-twisting sound of matter in the crucible of creation. Visions flashed before his eyes, a room in which a man sat engrossed with ancient scrolls, an army locked in desperate encounter with shapes of green and silver which fell only to rise again in spirals of red and gold. He saw ruined cities and heaps of mounded dead. A flower glowed in solitary splendor at the summit of a mountain.

The visions came even faster, a cell in which three men sat in filthy straw, a woman who casually brushed her mane of golden hair. A mummy rested in the masonry of a moldering wall. A ship drifted against a background of stars. Men moved over a board of ten million squares.

The voices.

"You yield, sister?"

"Not so, brother. My piece is not yet defeated."

"Yet surely it is only a matter of time? My hazard will conquer."

"Perhaps. But he must have his chance to win."

"And to escape?"

"That too, brother—if he can find himself."

"You think that he will?"

"We shall see, brother. We shall see."

Golden figures seated on a bowl of immensity playing a game of such complexity that his mind could not assimilate more than a fragment. The players of the Omphalos gone almost at once, lost in the mounting blur of visions which flashed stroboscopically before his eyes and all the time he was falling...falling...

To be spat like a morsel of dirt back through the ebon disc and onto the empty altar of Kanin.

15

THE temple was deserted. Carodyne rolled from the polished slab of the altar and stood trembling with delayed reaction. The sword was gone and he was naked, his body smeared with odorous slime, blood oozing from a dozen minor wounds. He ached with fatigue, his muscles sore and twitching with hyperstrain. His head throbbed and nausea gripped his stomach.

It had been no dream though the events had held all the elements of nightmare. He had really fought and hurt and even killed and he would have died in the space between dimensions if he had been a cowering sacrifice numbed with superstitious dread. If he had not had the aid of a forgotten magician who had inscribed symbols of power on the blade of a sword. If he had not thought to challenge and to cheat.

The nausea returned and he fought it, leaning against the altar and sucking air deep into his lungs. He would have been helpless had there been guards or even priests, but the vast chamber was empty of life. Natural enough, he thought, looking at the dull light of scattered torches, the winking gleam from the gemmed roof. Kanin had come and Kanin had fed and who could tell if the thing's hunger had been appeased? They had watched and then they had left, emptying the area before the gate of succulent life. Later, no doubt, the priests would return and other ceremonies begin. Before that happened he had to escape.

Wine stood on a shelf behind the ebon disc, rich liquid in clay urns sealed with mystic symbols. He broke the seals and drank, using more wine to wash his head and body. It was strong, the alcohol stinging where it touched his wounds, the sharp pain serving to eliminate some of his fatigue. He checked the votive offerings but could find nothing to serve as a weapon. The sword he had snatched had been the only one of its kind. Luck, he thought grimly. The unknown quantity which had enabled him to survive. The luck he still needed, for though he had escaped the death intended, men still waited outside the chamber and they could kill as effectively as any supposed god.

Quietly he moved down the length of the temple and paused before the great valves of the door. They were unlocked and moved easily on greased hinges. Through the gap he saw the annex, passages leading to rooms, other openings which could lead to the lower levels or to those above. He tensed, listening, but could hear nothing. Like an eel he slipped through the gap and into the annex.

And turned to meet the incredulous stare of two guards wearing temple plumage who stood to either side of the great doors.

Their amazement saved him. One fell immediately, choking from a ruptured larynx as the edge of Carodyne's left hand chopped at his throat. With his right he tore the guard's sword from its scabbard and ran to the second man. He was fast, almost too fast, steel rang and sparks flew bright in the dimness as the swords met, then Carodyne had swept his blade in a tight circle and thrust at the mouth opening to yell a warning. He felt the shock as the steel grated against teeth, driving through the gullet into the spine beyond. Tearing free the blade he raced back along the path the procession had taken.

There were too many turns, too many passages and blank doors. Baffled he slowed, hearing the sound of marching feet from ahead, springing into a side passage to crouch, chest heaving, as a party of guards passed almost within touching distance. They would find the dead and give the alarm. In a matter of minutes the temple would be alive with searching men ready to kill on sight. Time was running out.

He moved further down the side passage testing the doors. One yielded to the pressure of his hand and he slipped into a small chamber. A tiny lamp glowed against one wall and the air was close and heavy with perfume. On the bed a woman stirred, waking, rising wide-eyed at the sight of the naked stranger with the bloodstained sword.

Before she could scream Carodyne was on her, left hand clamped over her mouth, the point of the sword pricking her flesh.

"Quiet," he whispered. "I don't want to hurt you, but if you scream I'll kill you. Understand?"

She tried to nod.

"How do I get to the dungeons? Tell me and you won't get hurt."

She had expected the sword to penetrate her heart. Relief edged her words as he lifted the muffling hand.

"From this chamber move to the right. Turn left at the far passage. The way below lies behind the third door on the right." Her eyes grew wanton. "Is there anything else you'd like?"

Her silence. His left hand moved, the fingers digging into her throat, finding the great arteries which carried blood to the brain. He pressed until she slumped unconscious then moved quickly towards the door. His luck held. He heard a distant shout as he left the room, the clatter of running feet and then he was at the end of the passage and opening the third door on the right. A gust of noisome air rose from a flight of stairs from the foot of which came the clunk of metal. Cautiously he descended, sword poised for cut or thrust. Three guards sat at a rough table rolling dice.

"By Kanin, have you ever seen such luck?" A small, squat man with a pockmarked face slammed his fist on the table causing wine cups to jump and a small heap of coins to jingle. "Four times he has won with as many throws. Am I never going to win?"

A second man, tall, thin, moved with a clink of accouterments. "No man can win forever. Let us join against him."

The winner grinned as he rolled the dice between his calloused palms. "Two stakes or one it is all the same," he said cheerfully. "Bet what you like and let the gods decide. How much am I going to win this—" He broke off, losing his smile as Carodyne ran from the foot of the stairs.

Two strokes and it was over. The guards were unhelmeted and awkward as they tried to rise from the table. The pock-marked man gulped as he stared at the sword aimed at his throat, the split skulls of his two companions. He cringed as the blade moved closer.

"The dungeon," snapped Carodyne. "The cell holding the men taken in the battle. Where is it?" He saw the movement of the man's eyes as he glanced to where a door pierced the wall. "And the keys? Where are the keys?"

Sweat beaded the scarred face. "On a nail beyond the portal. Master! I beg you! Spare my life!"

Carodyne drew back the sword. His arm was trembling a little, death came too easily in this world, and dealing death something which could become a habit. And yet only a fool would leave an enemy at his rear.

"Please, master!" The man was shaking. "I have a wife, children who need me."

"Lead the way," said Carodyne. "If you're lying you'll regret it."

The man did not lie. Hostig roared a welcome as they came in sight of the cage.

"Mark! The gods have answered my prayers. You are alive."

Seyhat jerked open the door as the guard fumblingly opened the cell. He stepped outside the others at his heels. To Carodyne he said, "Lend me your sword."

"Why?"

"To kill the guard, of course. What else?"

"He lives," said Carodyne. "Strip him and lock him in the cell." He stepped to where the cage hung against the wall. The sword whined as he slashed at the fastening and freed the lock. The man inside remained silent, not stirring as Carodyne tore open the door. He looked at the congested face, the blank, staring eyes.

"He swallowed his tongue," said Albasar quietly. "We heard him do it. It was not a nice thing to hear."

A man choking to death on his own flesh would hardly make pleasant music. Carodyne turned, his face hard, hatred of the thing which possessed the girl giving him new strength.

To the others he said, "This place stinks. Let us get out of here."

Back in the guardroom Albasar poured wine from an urn into a cup and spread his hands over the surface, his lips moving in a silent incantation. Intently he peered into the container.

Carodyne said, "Can you figure a safe way for us to leave the city?"

Frowning the sorcerer shook his head. "There are shadows and strange patterns of shifting darkness. It is almost as if great sorcery was at war with itself. Perhaps your battle with Kanin is not yet over. Not easily does a god accept defeat. Tell me, was a promise made? A curse given? A threat of some kind?"

"Not that I remember."

"Then I must try again."

Carodyne moved restlessly where he stood at the foot of the stairs. He was uncomfortably aware of the passage of time, and yet to move without a plan was to invite capture.

Hostig grunted as he stretched in his too-small armor. "We are dressed as guards. Couldn't we simply walk from this place while pretending that Albasar is our prisoner?"

"You make it sound easy," said Seyhat. "Are the guards all fools? Is Iztima blind? Can dead men be left lying and no one ask questions? Mark has performed a miracle in releasing us from that cell and finding us weapons, but is he a magician that he can waft us all to safety with a spell?"

"I didn't say he was," grumbled the big northerner. "I only said we could take a chance."

"We'll be taking that anyway. But let's make sure it's a good one. If—" Seyhat broke off, staggering as the floor suddenly shifted beneath their feet. "By the gods! What was that?"

Hostig grabbed at the table as the tremor was repeated. "The earth demon stirs," he rumbled. "I have felt it before. The gods grant the walls don't fall about our ears."

Again the floor shifted, a deep rumble coming from far below. On the table cups danced and spilled their contents. Hostig snatched up the urn and half drained it.

"Let us run," he suggested. "In the confusion we could escape the city."

"With gold," added Seyhat, with a mercenary's instinct for loot. "There is plenty in the palace and jewels in the temple. We needn't leave empty-handed."

Albasar lifted a hand for silence. His eyes glowed as he stared into a puddle of spilled wine. It spread as a third tremor, milder, shook the floor.

"It is as I suspected, sorcery is at war with itself. Kanin is wreaking vengeance and none who served him is safe. The use of the secret arts is not to be undertaken without due regard for what it entails. For each spell there is a price which must be paid in full. Forces used must be counterbalanced by other forces in equal measure or the debt accumulates and the unwise practitioner runs the risk of being blasted by his own recoiling powers. The priests of Kanin have been too liberal in their use of magic. Now they must pay."

Carodyne frowned, trying to understand the concept in more familiar terms. The conservation of energy, he decided, the need to replace what was taken. A crude analogy but good enough.

"And Iztima? Will she also have to pay?"

"Yes. From Kanin she took great powers and used them as she would. Her evil has doomed her to inevitable destruction."

Carodyne said, quietly, "But she is not to blame. She is possessed by another entity. The mind of a woman called Mukalash."

"Mukalash?" Albasar looked his surprise. "I remember her. A strange creature who shunned the company of others. The old king retained her for reasons of charity and granted her last request to be interred in the manner she specified."

"And that was?"

"To be embalmed. To be sealed and buried so as to render the corpse inviolable. I thought nothing of it at the time. No one did. It was just the dying whim of an old, harmless woman."

"Harmless?" Seyhat slammed his hand hard on the table. "A sweet young girl made to suffer the pains of hell because of a vicious old hag! The men who have died because of it! If what Mark says is true she is more to be pitied than blamed."

"It's true," said Carodyne.

Hostig said, "No one doubts you, Mark. But is there no way in which the deed could be undone?"

Albasar slowly stirred the puddle of wine. "The creature possessing her body could be exorcised," he admitted. "It would take great sorcery and the powerful aid of amenable spirits, but it could be done—if we had possession of the original body."

"The mummy?" Carodyne frowned. "But you buried her. Surely you must know where she lies?"

"I did not and do not," corrected the sorcerer quietly. "She was interred by the priests of Kanin and they will hold fast to their secret. Once they lose it the bargain with Kanin is broken and they will lose their power and their hope of survival."

"Your own magic?"

"Is unable to penetrate the veil. Great spells and mighty sorcery have been used to build a wall I cannot break. I am sorry, Mark, but unless we can find the body the queen is doomed."

"Let her die then," rumbled Hostig. "The world is full of women."

"But none so lovely as Iztima, eh, my friend?" Seyhat stared shrewdly at Carodyne. "A prize worth the winning if won it can be."

"She's beautiful," admitted Carodyne. "But she's more than that. She is the queen of this city and could get us out of here alive. If we could rid her of the creature possessing her then we'd have nothing to worry about." He paused and added, "I've seen the body. It's somewhere within the temple. I'm sure of it."

"You have seen it?" Albasar leaned close. "Are you certain?"

A montage of visions, blurred, stroboscopic, spanning space and time yet each of them, he was convinced, a glimpse of reality. Carodyne frowned, trying to remember, seeing the mummy, the woman brushing her hair, the moldering stones of an ancient wall.

And other things. Stars, a ship, the awesome beauty of the Omphalos. The voices, whispering, the players who had used him as a pawn, were still using him to play their incomprehensible game.

A game which he had to play and win or die—and he had come so near to losing so many times. As he was near to losing now. Would lose unless they could find the body, the means to escape.

"Yes," he said. "I've seen it. In what you would call a vision. And it's in the temple somewhere—but I don't know exactly where."

"Knowledge is never lost," said Albasar. "It can be forgotten but always it remains and sorcery can find it no matter how deeply it is buried. A vision holds all things even though we may not be aware of them. If you have seen the body it will give me the guidance I lack. But I need your cooperation. You must trust me. You must place your soul in my hands." His hand lifted to touch the sigil tattooed on his forehead. "By Marash I swear that you will come to no harm."

Carodyne said, "What do you want me to do?"

"Sit facing me. Relax. Concentrate on my eyes. Follow the commands of my voice. Do not fight against my will."

Hypnotism, thought Carodyne, sitting. Well, why not? That was a magic he understood and if others chose to call it sorcery what was the difference? And he could trust the sorcerer, his life was at stake together with the rest.

He concentrated on the green eyes.

They grew larger, burning orbs of emerald fire which swelled to fill the world, the universe. A point of reflected light in each eye began to spin, to drift together, to merge in a gigantic wheel of glowing brilliance. From a vast distance he could hear a voice, two voices, but they seemed to have no relation to either himself or the magician. The murmurs died, the wheel spun even faster and suddenly he was sinking into an emerald sea. Time ceased and then he saw the wheel again, spinning, slowing, diminishing to become a spark, the double reflection of a torch in the sorcerer's eyes.

134

Carodyne drew a deep breath. The hypnotism he had known was nothing like this. "Is it done?"

"It is done." Albasar was shaken, his hands trembling as he thrust them within the sleeves of his robe.

"Well?" Hostig was impatient. "Have you the answer?"

"Yes," said Albasar. "Now I know where the body is to be found."

16

THE table danced again as they left the room, the walls creaking as if stone were sliding on stone, the air filling with a fine dust which caught at the throat and stung the eyes. Another tremor, the worst yet, and Carodyne wondered how many more the building could stand. Not many, he guessed, but as yet there had been none of the more destructive aspects of a normal earthquake, the focal point must be far out to sea or, perhaps, this wasn't a normal earthquake at all. The others obviously didn't think so. Albasar paused on the stairs, his lips moving in the construction of a spell, or perhaps he was praying to his god. Spell or prayer would be equally effective, thought Carodyne; no words could halt the forces of nature.

Not words as he knew them, he corrected himself. Here on this world, where gods were real or beasts that were called gods were real, who could tell?

He shook his head, irritated at his mental wanderings. The world was as it was and he had to take it as he found it. And he had been given evidence enough to show that magic, here, was something to be reckoned with.

Magic and something else.

From above came a dreadful screaming. It grew louder as

135

they climbed the stairs, louder still as they opened the door. Men raced down the passage outside, wild-eyed, faces distorted in frantic terror. A woman stood, shrieking, tearing at her naked arms until the flesh ran red with blood. On the marble floor something oozed in a widening puddle of red flecked with white, the feathered headdress of a priest grotesque in the center of a heap of clothing.

"The vengeance of Kanin," said Albasar quietly. "Already his servants die."

Feet pounded towards them. A squad of guards filled the passage ushering men and women before them like a flock of sheep. An officer shouted at their rear.

"All to the temple! Only by great sacrifice and humble worship can we hope to regain the grace of Kanin! To the temple!" He slowed as he drew abreast to the four men in the doorway. "You heard what I said. Hurry!"

He ran after his men. Albasar glanced down the cleared passage.

"So far the gods are with us," he said calmly. "The mummy lies in a niche cut into the wall of the old temple. No man now living knows how old it is and few remember that there are foundations on foundations. If we can make our way to it we shall not be disturbed."

Hostig growled as his big hand clamped around the hilt of his sword. "Let those who disturb us make their peace before they do. I've no mind to be taken and put back into a cell or used as a sacrifice. If we're caught we fight to the death. Agreed?"

"Let's not welcome death before it comes." Seyhat was practical. "And before you talk about killing those who disturb us we have to get where we're going. You and I will walk to either side of the sorcerer while Mark takes the lead. Any meeting us should take us for guards intent on our business. If not we can take care of them. But wait for Mark to give the word. Don't be too quick to use your sword."

"And don't try to collect any loot," said Carodyne. "That goes for the both of you. All right, Albasar, which way do we go?"

In a tight knot they moved down the passage, through an arch and into a small chamber. Temple guards stared as they passed through but made no effort to either question or stop the little party. Guided by the sorcerer's whisper Carodyne led the way from the chamber into another passage which widened into a vaulted hall lined with statues made of polished marble, each life-sized and each bearing a lance.

"The past rulers of Kedash," murmured Albasar. "May Marash grant that we live to add more to their number."

The vaulted hall gave onto a low place which branched to either side under a roof of diamond shaped panels bearing armorial signs. Carodyne turned to the left and came face to face with a half-dozen men wearing temple plumage.

Their officer said, "Hold! Where are you going?"

"Business. The High Priest—"

"Is busy in the temple." Suspicion narrowed the man's eyes. "What are you doing here? You belong in the dungeons and that armor—"

Carodyne hit him in the throat, snatching out his sword with his free hand. He sensed rather than saw the others swing into action, steel flashing, hitting, filling the air with the butcher-sounds of primitive combat. It was two to one, but the temple guards wanted to live while their opponents were willing to die rather than be taken. They died beneath a storm of edged metal.

"Quick!" Carodyne glared at the sorcerer. "Which way now?"

"Ahead, to the right at the far end, through the chamber and then left."

They ran from the shambles, swords red in their hands, sandals loud on the marble floor. A guard stared at them and ran, his spear falling behind him. Another, braver or stupider, lifted his weapon, the point veering as he tried to make up his mind which target to aim at. Hostig's thrown sword hit him in the face, Seyhat's cut his throat.

The chamber ended, yielding to a passage, a door, another room beyond which came the sound of a multitude of voices. The chant broke as a woman screamed, returned to the drone of priests. Dank air gushed past them as Albasar opened a hidden panel. Beyond lay a noisome darkness.

"Torches," rumbled Hostig. "We need light." He ran to

where flambeaux burned and returned, sword between his teeth, a flaring brand in each hand. "More?"

"No time."

Carodyne snatched one of the torches and thrust it through the opening. Stone stairs slimed with age fell sharply to a lower level. He ran down them, hearing the slam as Albasar closed the panel. A flat space, a landing, and then more stairs falling to a broad area flagged with chiseled stone. Vaulted roofs ran in every direction, their arches thick with cobwebs.

"We must go lower." Albasar quested like a dog, hands outstretched, his shadow monstrous in the flaring light. "Here, I think. No, here!" He pointed to a heavy slab of stone. "If that could be raised?"

Hostig handed him his torch and bent over the stone. He grunted as his fingers searched for a hold, cursing as he found none.

"Use your sword as a lever," snapped Carodyne. From above came the sound of muffled pounding. "Hurry!"

He tensed as the pounding increased. If the guards should find the panel, break it down, they would be caught like rats in a trap. Handing his torch to Seyhat he joined the big northerner.

Hostig had rammed his sword into a crack and was bearing down on the hilt. The blade bent as the stone lifted a little, bent still more and then snapped with a brittle sound.

"Try again," said Carodyne. "I'll use my sword. When it lifts shove your hilt in the crack and then use your hands. Ready?"

The stone lifted with a rasp of rusty hinges showing more stairs, worn, bright with encrustations. The torches burned low as they descended, Hostig lowering the slab back into place. Their voices sounded eerie in the muffling darkness.

"Few know of this place," said Albasar. "Only the priests of the temple and the students of ancient things. It will lead us to the place we need to find. Be careful of your heads— those who built it were smaller than men are now."

"Too small," grumbled Hostig as his helmet clashed against the roof. "How far must we travel?"

"At least we are safe here," mused Seyhat. Then added, "From men at least."

138

The passage lowered until they crawled almost on all fours. The floor was thick with dust which rose in clouds to catch at nose and throat, harsh, acrid and carrying a stench of decay. Carodyne felt something roll beneath his hand and stared at a bone in the guttering light. It was dark brown, fretted with the unmistakable signs of teeth, the marks too fresh for comfort.

He said, "Must we return this way?"

"No. There is another, easier to travel, but we had no chance to reach it from above." The sorcerer led the way to the right as the passage branched. "Almost we are there."

They emerged into a high-roofed area crusted with the deposits of uncounted years. Carodyne stretched and waved the torch to brighten the flame. In the light he saw the moldering wall of his vision. Albasar held out his hand.

"Give me a sword."

He held it loosely, both hands on the hilt, standing with his eyes closed and breathing deeply in a peculiar rhythm. The point of the sword lifted, weaved, steadied as he followed its direction. Dowsing, thought Carodyne, using the sword as another man might use a hazel twig, but where that other man would be searching for water the sorcerer was seeking a corpse.

"Here," he said finally. "Behind this stone."

Hostig attacked it together with Carodyne, both men straining, using swords as levers to wrest the stone from its bed. It fell with a crash and a rising cloud of dust. Beyond it lay the square end of a metal coffin. In it lay the wrapped body of a mummy.

Carodyne lifted his sword. "We have to be sure." With deft strokes he ran the edge over the wrappings and looked down at the sere and withered body of a crone.

"Mukalash," said Albasar quietly. "Is this she who inhabits the body of Iztima?"

"That's the thing I saw. Can you free the girl of her possession?"

"I can, but not here. The stone has absorbed much of her sorcerous power and there are spells impossible to negate while in this area. In my old chambers I have many articles

139

and objects of value. The symbols inscribed on the floor will be of worth and there are scrolls it would be wise to consult."

Carodyne frowned. "Your old quarters? Here in the temple?"

"They are not far. And there is a secret way shorter than that by which we came. It is a risk, I know, but one which must be taken. Sorcery of the highest order is involved and there will be only one chance of success."

"Then let us get on with it," said Hostig impatiently. "I don't like this place. If we're going to die let's do it where there is light and air and men around us. Not in a tomb with a coffin."

"Which we must take with us," reminded Seyhat. "Mark?"

Carodyne shrugged and to Albasar said, "We'll do it your way. Take the lead."

The coffin had an inner shell of light wood treated with something which had turned it to a surprising hardness. They closed it and lifted it, supporting it as they climbed endless stairs, pausing often to catch their breath, the torches now little more than glowing embers. Even the embers died before they reached the upper levels and they fumbled in total darkness until Albasar halted, his hands rasping at a wall.

Light shone around them, soft, warm, almost blinding after the stygian darkness. It spread as a panel swung wide showing a narrow passage lit from torches set behind panes of translucent crystal. Carodyne followed the sorcerer as he stepped into the passage, the other two grunting as they maneuvered the coffin through the narrow opening.

"To the left," said Albasar softly. "Then right at the end of the passage. A hundred paces and we shall be in my chambers. Once inside my sorcery will protect us."

Carodyne said, "Can't it now?"

"I have done what I can, but the spells are weak and of little value. It would be best to hurry."

Good advice at any time especially when moving through an area filled with searching men. Carodyne stepped ahead, his feet creating little sounds from the tessellated floor. Echoes rose about him, magnified by the confines of the passage, the labored breathing of the others, the clink of metal, the rustle of the sorcerer's robe. His skin crawled with anticipated dangers; a single guard would be able to give the alarm, a handful would have them at their mercy. He lifted his sword, the blade bent but still serviceable as a club if nothing else.

They reached the end of the passage and turned to the right to where the chambers of Albasar offered safety.

Waiting for them were a score of men.

17

THEY were tall, hard, the pick of the temple guard. More joined them, running, swords naked in their hands to surround the coffin and the men who carried it. Carodyne tried to jump clear and felt the prick of steel at his throat. He froze, knowing that he tasted death, that a single step, a movement, would cost him his life. A hand snatched the bent sword from his fingers.

Bleakly Carodyne looked beyond the guards to where a door stood in shadows. Symbols marked it, an intricate pattern of lines and curves reminiscent of electronic circuitry. Albasar's chamber which offered safety. The refuge they had been unable to reach. A gamble, he thought, and one they had lost.

From the shadows stepped the High Priest of Kanin, Iztima at his side.

"Your warning devices did not fail you, my queen," he said. "What is your pleasure with these men?"

"Death," she said coldly. "It is long overdue. Kill them and have done with it."

Taneft raised a hand as if in gentle admonition. "Certainly, death," he agreed. "But a man can die in many ways. What manner of end should be meted out to those who have

141

caused such disturbance? To be roasted slowly over a flame? To be dismembered under spells so that they live as things of horror? To watch as they are flayed or dipped slowly into baths of acid?"

She said, again, "Kill them. Do it now."

"Wait!" said Carodyne and then, more evenly, "Wouldn't that be rather a waste?"

He felt the sword dig into his flesh, the blood as it ran warm over his throat and chest, the warning growl of the guard. He ignored both the pain and the warning.

"Listen," he said loudly. "Be logical about this. I was sacrificed to Kanin. I fought the god and I won. Fighting him I learned certain things which might interest you. If you kill me you will never learn what they are."

Another gamble but life was full of them, calculated chances in order to survive. If her curiosity was stronger than her blood lust, he would, if nothing else, gain a little time.

Quickly he added, "One of them was how to find the coffin. Another was how to regain his favor. A third was how to blast you all where you stand."

He felt the recoil of the surrounding guards, the instinctive withdrawing from something they regarded with superstitious dread. He was bluffing but they couldn't be sure of that. And he had fought with their god and won.

He heard Hostig's dull rumble. "Now, while they are unprepared. Now!"

Albasar said, quietly, "Struggle not. Our hour is yet to come."

"You think so?" Taneft thrust himself forward, his face hard with anger. "Do you hope that your weak god will replace the mighty Kanin? I tell you that if half this city needs to be sacrificed I will regain his favor. Once again he will give us power and once again he will grace his priests with secrets unknown to lesser men."

"A god does not return, false priest. Not even a thing as vile as that you worship. Not to restore grace to those who have served him ill. I tell you that you and yours face a terrible end. Plainly I can read your doom."

"Silence!" Taneft raised his hand in a mystical gesture. Albasar stared his contempt as the gesture had no effect.

142

"You see, priest? No longer are you able to summon sorcerous power. Soon you must pay the debt you have accumulated. I say that I would not be in your place for the wealth of a world."

"Speak again and the hilt of a sword shall smash your teeth!" Taneft fought to control his anger. To the guards he said, "Take them to the temple. To the great hall. Bring the coffin with you."

"No!" Iztima was quick to protest. "I don't care what you do with the prisoners so long as they die, but the coffin must be taken to my quarters. Guards! See to it."

They hesitated, inflaming her anger.

"Guards! Obey!"

"They belong to the temple," said Taneft coldly. "Dedicated men who obey only my commands for fear that their ghosts will howl for an eternity in outer darkness. And don't try to numb me with your magic," he added sharply as she lifted her hands. "Your sorcery will be as powerless as mine. Now come! To the temple! We have delayed too long."

Albasar fell into step beside Carodyne as they were ushered down the passage. The guards were uneasy, giving them plenty of room so that they walked in a small oasis of privacy.

Quietly, almost whispering, he said, "When you spoke of powers given you by Kanin did you mean what you said?"

Carodyne shook his head.

"And yet you spoke more truth than you may have guessed. When I looked into your mind to discover where the body of Mukalash was hidden I learned that you are not as normal men. No such could ever have bested Kanin. In you reside great powers and a mystery I cannot comprehend. You are here and yet you are not here. A part of your mind belongs to another place of great magic and sorcerous achievement which makes insignificant the powers I command. And yet that magic is barred to you. Is that correct?"

Science, discovery, a technology which had given men the stars. And yet, in this world, the wave of a hand and a few muttered words seemed to have more effect than what he knew. Like a genius in a cell, thought Carodyne bitterly. A man who knew the atomic structure of the metal which held him—but who lacked a saw to get himself out.

"Reality," continued the sorcerer, "is the impact of the world on our senses. A trained adept can so change it that the touch of heated iron will not burn his skin. This I have seen and can, in some measure, do. Yet we are all prisoners of the world in which we were born so that to all men reality will appear to be the same." He paused and added, softly, "But if a man should have come from another place would his reality be that of others?"

"You're saying something," said Carodyne. "What?"

"I need your powers," said Albasar. "I admit it. Despite what I said to Taneft his sorcery is still very strong. I was able to baffle his minor spell but in the temple Kanin may well listen to his pleas. If so we all die in torment. But if, with your help, I could diminish his power, then all could be well."

"If you want my help you can have it," said Carodyne. "But what can I do?"

"Sharpen your mind. Think of that other place. Make it real. By so doing you will create confusion and perhaps something more. Gods exist only because of the belief of their worshipers."

Find yourself, thought Carodyne. Find yourself and find escape. But how? He touched the wound on his throat and looked at the blood on his hand. Real or not the sword had cut his skin. Could he stand and convince himself that the weapon did not exist? Was the Omphalos only a dream?

No dream, he thought, remembering. A different reality, perhaps, but certainly no dream. And a reality which, for him, might end all too soon.

Gongs throbbed as they entered the great hall by a side door, emerging to stand between the dais and the congregation. The brazen clamor rose again as they halted before the altar, dying in murmurings against the vaulted roof. The air reeked of incense and the sharp taint of freshly spilled blood. Red-armed priests had turned the area into a shambles, the ripped bodies of sacrificial victims piled in an untidy heap to one side.

Carodyne glanced at the ebon disc. From it came a wave of savage ferocity. He could sense it hanging in the air, almost angible with menace, frightening with the threat of destruction to come.

Kanin was behind it, lurking at the threshold of the gate, watching, waiting, unwilling to be appeased.

Hostig's voice rumbled as he lowered the coffin. "Let us snatch swords and do what we can. If this is the end let us die like men."

"Patience," whispered Albasar. "Do nothing rash."

Taneft heard him and turned, his face distorted with rage, his hand lifted as if to strike. Before the blow could fall one of his acolytes came thrusting his way through the guards to bow before the High Priest.

"My lord, save us! We have offered a dozen virgins and twice as many others, but still Kanin ignores us. What more should we do?"

"Pray," snapped Taneft. "And wait. I shall attend to what needs to be done."

"Soon, my lord?"

"Man, you forget yourself! Remember to whom you speak!" As the man backed, groveling, the High Priest turned to Carodyne. "When you were taken you made certain claims. If true they could bring you high reward. Quickly now—tell me how to regain the favor of Kanin."

Carodyne met his eyes. "And in return?"

"Your life."

"As a slave? To be spent cooped up in a cage?"

"As a captain of my guard with women and gold and things of comfort. Aid me now and you will have no cause to regret it. This I swear by the god I serve."

Iztima called from where she stood beside the coffin. "No! The man must die!"

"Be silent, woman!"

"Taneft, you talk to your queen. Remember it!"

"I am the High Priest of Kanin. In this place my authority is supreme. Do not meddle with matters you cannot understand." And then to Carodyne, "Answer me quickly. Will you do as I ask or will you die in torment?"

Carodyne smiled, apparently relaxed, inwardly a knot of tension. The seed he had sown had borne fruit in the dissen-

145

sion between Iztima and Taneft if nothing else. But it was a fruit which could turn sour if he waited too long.

"You leave me no choice," he said casually. "Give me what you promised and I will do as you say."

"Later, after Kanin has been appeased. What must I do?"

Carodyne hesitated, tempted to order the withdrawal of the guards, a sword to be used for some magical purpose, Iztima to stand beside him as a hostage, but he knew the man would never agree. Taneft was no fool. Only desperation had made him ask for help, that and the fact that Carodyne had actually met and bested the god. Proof of the knowledge he claimed to hold.

From somewhere a man screamed in an extremity of pain.

"Quickly!" Taneft was sweating, his eyes haunted. "Speak or die!"

"You are the High Priest," said Carodyne. "You know the rituals, the ceremonies which need to be done. Have them prepared. I shall communicate with Kanin and do what I must. What I promise you must fulfill. Fail me and we both die."

Superstition, but no one who believed in sorcery could be without it. Not even Albasar. Carodyne glanced at the sorcerer and caught the message in his eyes. Now was the time for him to do as the other had asked. To sharpen his mind. To think of other places, other worlds. To try, in some small way, to change reality.

But how?

He walked to the altar and stood before it, turning so as to see the congregation. A sea of faces all bearing the stamp of terror. The guards, bright in barbaric lighting with their armor and plumes and shining swords. The priests, the queen, Albasar, the two who had traveled with him so long, Taneft—all figments of imagination.

They were not real. They could not be real. They were characters in a transdimensional sensorama together with the vaulted hall with its gemmed roof, the tessellated floor, the heap of victims sprawled like broken dolls to one side. The blood was paint used to give effect. He had seen it all before.

He did not belong here.

146

This was not his world.

It had never been his world.

He belonged to where ships traversed the stars and science imposed a firm discipline on natural law. Where atoms yielded their energy and gods were dreams of poets and fantasies to amuse children. Where magicians and queens and barbarians with swords and spears illustrated recreational tapes or lived as magnetic stresses in machines designed to beguile with exotic dreams. Where words of power were equations and symbols were circuits and demons were the pulse of electrons and sorcery was science and magicians those who studied it. Where queens and kings and castles and warriors were nothing more than pieces set out on a board of tessellated squares.

From behind blew a gelid wind.

It passed him, going around him, through him as if he did not exist. He could see it stir particles on the floor catching at the flames of the torches and causing them to gutter but he could not feel it at all. There was no pressure against his back. Nothing to chill or to drone. A wind without substance discernible only by its effect.

Albasar straightened, lifting his arms, his voice like a throbbing organ as he uttered a string of archaic syllables. Priests moved forward to silence him, slowing as they approached to halt finally in attitudes of helpless despair. The guards stood as if stricken to stone.

Amusing, thought Carodyne. But something was out of place. A thing which should be corrected.

In the coffin something moved.

It flickered with a skein of light, burning, fading to burn again, shimmering with variegated color. The withered body stirred, seemed to come suddenly alive, clawed hands lifting as if in desperate appeal. The hands blossomed with flesh, grew young, firm and vibrant with health. The face filled, the bones of the skull disappearing beneath layers of fat and tissue and radiant skin. Hair sprouted to fall in a golden cloud about rounded shoulders, the succulent contours of high, proud breasts.

And then, abruptly, the resemblance of youth vanished and the body was as before.

147

Carodyne frowned.

Again the thing in the coffin moved, twisting as if trying to escape from the confines of the box. Over it colors flickered in a stroboscopic pattern so that at one moment it was the sere and dessicated figure of a corpse, the next the body of a young and lovely girl. Abruptly it glowed with a dull red fire and, in his mind, Carodyne heard a frenzied screaming.

"No! Dear god, no! Great Kanin remembered our pact!"

The wailing died, shrilling like the grate of a nail over slate as, within the coffin, fire rose to consume every scrap of what it had contained.

"It is done." Albasar lowered his arms. "The spirit of Mukalash has gone and Iztima is free of the thing which possessed her."

She stood beside the High Priest, hands pressed to her face, swaying a little as if about to faint. Then, as Carodyne watched, she lowered her hands and stared directly into his eyes. A beautiful woman, he thought, holding the most ancient magic of all. And, as he looked at her, the scene became more real. He could smell the odors of blood and incense, hear little sounds, the rasp of sandals on the tessellated floor, the gusting sigh of indrawn breath.

The torchlight flared. A guard moved with a click of accrouterments. Another dropped his hand to the hilt of his sword, his eyes wild with terror of the unknown.

And, again, the gust of gelid wind.

"Beware, mortals! Now you must pay!"

A voice, cold as ice, searing with mental impact from the thing which lurked before the gate. A crouching beast like a mutated scorpion vile against the stars. Kanin eager for revenge.

A priest screamed and slumped in a puddle of ooze. Another followed. Three more burst into columns of smoking flame. The great hall rang to the shrieks as those who had served the entity paid for the favors they had received.

The High Priest changed.

Where he had stood swayed a thing of horror, blood and fluids streaming from a carmined tree hung with the repulsive fruit of naked organs. Unseen powers had turned him inside out, reversing his body as a man would strip off a lexible glove. From the midst of the ghastly thing came the ongueless mewing of a creature mad with pain.

Carodyne leaped towards a guard, snatched the sword from nerveless fingers, swung it with a flashing glitter of steel. The edge hit, dragged, burst free as the tormented priest fell in two halves, silent in merciful death.

As the body fell Carodyne turned and ran towards the disc. Again he swung the blade, twice more. The first time the edge slashed at something like smoke. The second rang harshly on a brittle surface. The third and both the sword and the disc shattered in a rain of fragments.

He looked at a mirror.

18

IT was a circle of silvery brightness, smooth, a skin of perfect reflection. It hung between the surround of gilded metal, edged by fragments of shattered stone, the activating principle of the gate which had enabled Kanin to penetrate this world from its own dimension. In it he saw himself.

Himself?

A stranger. A barbarian dressed in primitive armor, stained and flecked with dirt and blood, the face a taut mask of savage determination. Wonderingly he lifted his right hand to touch his cheek and the image did the same.

The right hand?

A mirror would have reflected his image, but in reverse. This was no ordinary reflecting surface. In it he could see himself, had found himself, perhaps. What was it Albasar had said? Find the mirror of truth? Was this it?

He reached out and touched it, feeling a prickle beneath his fingers. He pressed harder and felt a sudden pull, a moment of nausea. Startled he looked out at the great hall. Iztima leaning towards him, hands outstretched, Albasar arms lifted, his lips moving in an incantation. He had no memory of turning. He had done nothing but reach towards his image but, somehow, he had become that image. He was in the field of the gate looking at the interior of the temple.

A step and he could be among them.

He did not take it. Instead he turned and looked down a narrowing tunnel blotched with a patch of light at the far end. A tunnel which could be only as long as the mirror was thick which was no thickness at all. But all things were relative and an image could have no thickness, an infinity of them piled one on the other would have no more depth than one. But he was not wholly an image and the mirror was more than just a reflecting surface.

He began to run down the tunnel.

It was as if he raced in a dream. His legs moved, his heart pounded, the breath rasped in his lungs but the patch of light seemed to come no closer, the silvery sides of the tunnel did not appear to move. Yet he was moving, he was certain of it, running and covering microscopic distances with every step. Enough of them and he would reach the end. He had to reach the end.

It was his only promise of escape.

An eternity of effort and he fell into the patch of light, rolling to rest face down on a bed of soft, sweet-smelling grass. A gentle breeze cooled his body and, after a long while, he turned and looked at an azure sky and the drifting shapes of little white clouds. From somewhere came the thin chiming of bells and he rose looking for signs of life. He saw nothing but trees on which hung tinkling fruits. He turned and saw a grassy slope rising to a smooth crest tufted with clumps of vegetation. There was no sign of the tunnel down which he had run.

Another world, Earth perhaps, the grass was the same, the sky and the clouds, and the trees with their tinkling fruits could have been an import from some exotic world. The fields and gardens held many varieties of similar plants.

Home then, free of the Omphalos, set down on the planet of his birth.

Carodyne filled his lungs with the scented air and began to climb the slope. He was probably in a reservation, one of the vast areas set aside for sport and recreation, but there would be paths and roads and places to rest. He would find one and bathe and eat and sleep for a while. He would make his way to a city and familiar things and begin to live again as a civilized man.

As he neared the crest a man stepped from a clump of trees.

He was tall, dressed in faded denim which he had ornamented with bright seeds and tassels of leaves. He carried a long wooden pole with a sharpened end, the shaft carved in an abstract design. His hands were large, the palms broad and the fingers blunt, and both hands and face were tanned a deep brown. His hair was long and held by a fillet of woven grass. He had no beard and his eyes were crinkled and vividly blue.

He said, "Hello, there!"

"Hello," answered Carodyne.

"You're a stranger," said the man. "I don't see many strangers. Most of the time I'm alone but I've got used to it and, to tell you the truth, I'd rather have it that way. What's your name?"

Mark gave it. "And yours?"

"Conway. Bill Conway. You look as if you'd had a rough time."

"You could call it that."

"You look rough, but I've seen worse. And then, again, I've seen a lot better. I guess it's all the luck of the game."

"The game?"

"That's right. The game."

Carodyne looked at him. Eccentrics were not unknown on Earth and many of them lived in the reservations content to make their own lives and find their own peace. Conway could be one. But a man would have to be very eccentric indeed not to pass more comment on a man who wore primitive armor soiled with blood and dirt.

151

He said, "What do you do here? Are you a warden?"

"Well, yes, in a manner of speaking I guess you could ca'
me that."

"Then could you direct me to a hostel?"

Conway chuckled. "That's a hard one. I guess you coul
turn left at the crest and head for the shimmer. Or turn righ
and go down the gully into the blur. Or there's always th
rainbow. I guess one of them might take you where you wan
to go. Of course I can't be sure about that, I've never bee
myself, but you could always try."

"And over the crest?"

"You don't go over the crest."

"You'd stop me?"

"Well, now," said Conway seriously, "I'd try. I'd do m
best and, if I say so myself, my best is pretty good. I'd sur
hate to do it but if you insisted then I'd have to stop you. I
your condition it shouldn't be too hard."

A madman, but a dangerous one armed as he was witl
his crude spear. A self-appointed guardian of what lay ove
the hill—or a man set on guard.

The thought was disturbing. Carodyne said, "I don't wan
to go over the crest, but can I take a look?"

"Just a look?"

"That's right. Will you let me do that?"

"Yes," said Conway. "There's no rule against that. Bu
only look, mind."

They reached the crest and Carodyne halted and stare
at madness. A formless blur of mist and coils and achin
emptiness. A vastness which surged and roiled and sparkle
with darting glimmers of light. A chaotic ocean which lappe
at the crest where it ended a few yards from where he stood
He turned, shuddering, eager to rest his eyes on green an
blue and fluffy whiteness.

But the colors were a deception. This wasn't Earth
He hadn't been returned to his own world. He hadn'
escaped. He was still a prisoner of the Omphalos and tha
was unfair.

Or was it?

He had found himself, but what had he really found? A
image on a screen, a thing without real depth or substance

And a man was more than a superficial reflection. He had seen how he looked and perhaps a little more than that but it hadn't been enough.

"You look bad," said Conway. "Maybe you should sit awhile."

Carodyne said, dully, "How long have you been here?"

"Here?"

"In the Omphalos."

"What is the Omphalos?"

The question no one could answer. Perhaps it was alive in some way unimaginable to the normal universe. A single creature or more than one like the bees which went to make up a hive or the cells of a normal body. And yet it was more than that. There was a kind of pattern so that men could live on worlds which logically couldn't exist. He thought of what he had seen, the turmoil of primeval matter, forces and light interspersed with darkness and twisting clouds.

Chaos as it could have been in the very beginning. A complex of rebellious forces which obeyed no set laws, changing in a kaleidoscope of varying cause and effect, forming new relationships, destroying old, a madness to anyone used to discipline and regular order.

But that was not the answer. Not the whole answer. Could an ant understand the complexity of a skyscraper? A fly the mechanisms of a ship of space?

To Conway he said, again. "How long have you been here?"

"Well now, that's hard to say. A long time, I guess. I just don't think about it. I eat the fruits and sleep when I want and walk a little and sometimes I meet a stranger and we talk awhile. And I make things." He hefted his spear and touched the adornments on his faded denim. "I like making things. Not big things, you understand, but small things."

"And before you were here, what then?"

"That was a bad time and I don't like to think about it much."

"Try," urged Carodyne. "You were born somewhere. Where?"

"A bad place. Things were hard and I couldn't get along.

153

They took me and did things to me." The big hands trembled a little on the wooden shaft of the spear. "It was a bad time."

On a world perhaps similar to Earth, or it could even have been Earth; the place he had was like what Carodyne remembered. Green grass and a blue sky and the whiteness of cloud. A man who perhaps had been unable to adjust or who had different frames of reference from those around him. A crazy man, a psychotic who had been shipped out of the neatly arranged society of an old and civilized world and sent to another planet.

Had his ship fallen into the Omphalos?

Entering it a sane man would go mad—would a mad man go sane?

Was insanity the inability to accept the reality of others and, if so, could mental health only be achieved by fashioning an individual world? As Conway had done?

The man did not look insane. In fact he looked calm and pleased and utterly content, but if he lived in a world of his own making that was surely to be expected. And would there be other worlds, tiny spheres fashioned by others strung throughout the Omphalos like pearls on a string?

And, if so, what of the Players? Who and what could they be?

An ant, thought Carodyne bleakly, trying to understand the complexity of a city.

Conway said, "Well now, you've had your look over the crest and I guess you'll be wanting to get along."

"Yes," said Carodyne. "I suppose so."

There was no point in staying here and no real place for him despite the green grass, the blue sky and fluffy clouds. This was not Earth or any world he knew. This was only a part of another man's reality fashioned out of chaos and he was a stranger, an interloper, perhaps.

"You know how it is," said Conway. "A man gets used to his ways. But if you want to visit again you're always welcome."

"Thank you," said Carodyne. "I'll remember that."

"To sit awhile and rest and talk a little."

154

"You're a good man."

"I try to be," said Conway. "It isn't always easy. There are too many who won't let you be as you want. But not here, though. Everything's fine here."

As long as there weren't others around. As long as you didn't question and probe and look for answers. As long as you could simply accept. But that was not Carodyne's way.

"I'll be moving on," he said. "Which way should I take?"

"Well now, as I told you, there's the shimmer or the blur. But you came from up the slope so I guess the rainbow would be best. It's just along here aways."

It was an arc hardly visible against the greenery, a barely seen semicircle of color. Conway lifted his spear as they reached it and Carodyne raised his hand in return farewell. For a moment longer he looked at the grass and the sky and clouds and the calm contentment on the other man's face. And then he turned and took a single step forward.

And halted.

He stood in a shattered ring of stone facing a great hall lit by dancing flames. Before him stood Albasar, arms uplifted, lips moving in an incantation. Iztima stood beside the sorcerer, facing the shattered disc, hands outstretched. Beyond her he could see the assembled congregation, the guards, the waxen faces of the remaining priests. Behind him stood nothing but the great blocks of an ancient wall.

Nothing had changed, he thought dully. No time had passed. He had walked to the disc and broken it and then had reached forward. Perhaps he had flickered a little as the screen collapsed, but that could have been all. His journey, his talk with Conway, his glimpse of the turmoil beyond the crest had taken no time at all. Had it all been in his mind?

And, if so, did it matter?

This was his world and he had to live in it. A place of violence and war and savage death. He stepped down and walked to where the woman waited. The queen he could take.

155

Would take as he would hold the city. As he would fight until he won.

A pawn, he thought. A piece in a game. But even in chess a pawn could rise above its limitations. And if it could do that in a simple game devised by men how much more powerful could it be in the universe of the Omphalos?

Big enough and powerful enough to sweep the board, perhaps.

And, after the board, the Players themselves.

In the Omphalos all things were possible.

From planet Earth
you will be able to
communicate with other worlds—
just read—

SCIENCE FICTION

THE GODS THEMSELVES by Isaac Asimov	23756	$1.95
BLACK HOLES edited by Jerry Pournelle	23962	$2.25
THE NAKED SUN by Isaac Asimov	24243	$1.95
BALLROOM OF THE SKIES by John D. MacDonald	14143	$1.75
DAUGHTER OF IS by Michael Davidson	04285	$1.75
EARTH ABIDES by George Stewart	23252	$1.95
THE JARGOON PARD by Andre Norton	23615	$1.95
STAR RANGERS by Andre Norton	24076	$1.95
THE SEVEN DEADLY SINS OF SCIENCE FICTION Edited by: Isaac Asimov, Charles G. Waugh, and Martin H. Greenberg	24349	$2.50

Buy them at your local bookstore or use this handy coupon for ordering.

COLUMBIA BOOK SERVICE (a CBS Publications Co.)
32275 Mally Road, P.O. Box FB, Madison Heights, MI 48071

Please send me the books I have checked above. Orders for less than
5 books must include 75¢ for the first book and 25¢ for each additional book to cover postage and handling. Orders for 5 books or
more postage is FREE. Send check or money order only.

Cost $_____   Name _____

Sales tax*_____   Address _____

Postage_____   City _____

Total $_____   State _____ Zip _____

*The government requires us to collect sales tax in all states except
AK, DE, MT, NH and OR.

This offer expires 1 September 81   8102

CLASSIC BESTSELLERS
from FAWCETT BOOKS

THE GHOST WRITER	24322	$2.75
by Philip Roth		
IBERIA	23804	$3.50
by James A. Michener		
THE ICE AGE	04300	$2.25
by Margaret Drabble		
ALL QUIET ON THE WESTERN FRONT	23808	$2.50
by Erich Maria Remarque		
TO KILL A MOCKINGBIRD	08376	$2.50
by Harper Lee		
SHOW BOAT	23191	$1.95
by Edna Ferber		
THEM	23944	$2.50
by Joyce Carol Oates		
THE SLAVE	24188	$2.50
by Isaac Bashevis Singer		
THE FLOUNDER	24180	$2.95
by Gunter Grass		
THE CHOSEN	24200	$2.25
by Chaim Potok		
THE SOURCE	23859	$2.95
by James A. Michener		

Buy them at your local bookstore or use this handy coupon for ordering.

COLUMBIA BOOK SERVICE (a CBS Publications Co.)
32275 Mally Road, P.O. Box FB, Madison Heights, MI 48071

Please send me the books I have checked above. Orders for less than 5 books must include 75¢ for the first book and 25¢ for each additional book to cover postage and handling. Orders for 5 books or more postage is FREE. Send check or money order only.

Cost $_____   Name _____

Sales tax*_____   Address _____

Postage_____   City _____

Total $_____   State _____ Zip _____

*The government requires us to collect sales tax in all states except AK, DE, MT, NH and OR.

This offer expires 1 September 81   8105

NEW FROM POPULAR LIBRARY

HAWKS   04620 $2.95
by Joseph Amiel

LOVE IS JUST A WORD   04622 $2.95
by Johannes Mario Simmel

NIGHT THINGS   04624 $2.25
by Thomas F. Monteleone

THE FOURTH WALL   04625 $2.25
by Barbara Paul

SCIENCE FICTION ORIGINS   04626 $2.25
Edited by William F. Nolan,
and Martin H. Greenberg

SAGA OF THE PHENWICK WOMEN #34,
URSALA THE PROUD   04627 $1.95
by Katheryn Kimbrough

Buy them at your local bookstore or use this handy coupon for ordering.

COLUMBIA BOOK SERVICE (a CBS Publications Co.)
32275 Mally Road, P.O. Box FB, Madison Heights, MI 48071

Please send me the books I have checked above. Orders for less than
5 books must include 75¢ for the first book and 25¢ for each additional book to cover postage and handling. Orders for 5 books or
more postage is FREE. Send check or money order only.

Cost $_____   Name _____

Sales tax*_____   Address _____

Postage_____   City _____

Total $_____   State _____ Zip _____

*The government requires us to collect sales tax in all states except
AK, DE, MT, NH and OR.

This offer expires 1 September 81   8098

NEW FROM FAWCETT CREST

DOMINO   24350 $2.75
by Phyllis A. Whitney

CLOSE TO HOME   24351 $2.50
by Ellen Goodman

THE DROWNING SEASON   24352 $2.50
by Alice Hoffman

OUT OF ORDER   24353 $2.25
by Barbara Raskin

A FRIEND OF KAFKA   24354 $2.50
by Isaac Bashevis Singer

ALICE   24355 $1.95
by Sandra Wilson

MASK OF TREASON   24356 $1.95
by Anne Stevenson

POSTMARKED THE STARS   24357 $2.25
by Andre Norton

Buy them at your local bookstore or use this handy coupon for ordering.

COLUMBIA BOOK SERVICE (a CBS Publications Co.)
32275 Mally Road, P.O. Box FB, Madison Heights. MI 48071

Please send me the books I have checked above. Orders for less than 5 books must include 75¢ for the first book and 25¢ for each additional book to cover postage and handling. Orders for 5 books or more postage is FREE. Send check or money order only.

Cost $_____   Name _____

Sales tax*_____ Address _____

Postage_____   City _____

Total $_____   State _____ Zip _____

* The government requires us to collect sales tax in all states except AK, DE, MT, NH and OR.

This offer expires 1 September 81   8096